And Then She Remembered

Beca Lewis

Perception Publishing

Contents

One

Ron Page had made them famous. None of them liked it. All of them prayed that a bigger news cycle would come around and the world would forget them and move on. Still, they knew that the likelihood was minuscule that people would forget that for years a serial killer had lived amongst them.

But at least they could do their best not to fan the flames. None of them responded to requests for interviews or posted on social media. The Ruby Sisters pulled in, closed ranks, and decided to wait it out.

And after Judith asked them to, the town of Spring Falls did the same. Never had Judith been as proud of her town because she only had to ask once. She invited everyone she knew—which was most of the town—to meet in April's empty house.

Judith stood at the front of the room, red hair flaming, and asked that they honor one of their own and protect April and their town. All the Ruby Sisters stood beside Judith, hands clasped, faces pale but determined. Except for April. April wasn't there, and that made what happened even more real.

"We are a community," Judith had said. "If something bad happens to any of us, we stand by one another."

Booker Morris stood in the back of the room, quietly watching, but everyone knew that he, as the Chief of Police, supported Judith's request.

"If you know anything that will help, please share it with the appropriate person," Judith said. "They will take it from there. This is not just one woman's tragedy. It is all of ours. You know you can come to me anytime if you are in trouble, and I will do what I can to help.

"And I know you will help April now by not gossiping and spreading rumors. By turning away requests from the media to dramatize what happened here."

Booker had watched the crowd as somehow Judith worked her magic. The worry and fear etched on the faces of many of the people in the room had begun to dissolve. Some faces reflected relief. Others sorrow. But Booker thought Judith had done it—diffused the bomb that Ron Page had thrown into their town.

After Judith spoke, the Ruby Sisters moved through the crowd, talking, hugging, and soothing. Booker watched them all as they worked the room, but his eyes kept returning to Marsha. He had noticed how Marsha would often look away when Ron's name was brought up in a conversation. Marsha's face would pale, and she'd glance to the side or look down at her hands, fidgeting in her lap. Booker knew that Judith, too, had noticed Marsha's reactions. Sooner or later, they'd get to the bottom of it.

But that day, all they all wanted was for Spring Falls to return to the quiet, comfortable, almost unknown town they knew and loved. And for April to find some peace and come back to them.

Harry the Hawk did what he had done all his life. He blended into the crowd. It was easy this time because everyone's eyes were on the tall, red-haired woman speaking at the front of the room, urging restraint and kindness.

Even if they weren't watching the woman, Harry knew that now that he was this old, it was even easier to become invisible. No one would notice him hidden in the back of the room. Over the years, his once blond hair had thinned into little wisps and his tall, lean body stooped over as he leaned more heavily onto his cane than necessary.

He was a nobody in this crowd, just as he wanted to be. As he always wanted to be. To his friends and enemies, he was Harry the Hawk, known for his keen awareness and ability to focus on a problem and resolve it. To everyone else, he didn't exist.

It had been a long time since he had found himself surrounded by people, because showing up in person was something he rarely did anymore. He had people who showed up for him. However, this time was different. Time was running out, and he had some debts to pay before he left this earth.

Harry was not afraid of being recognized. No one knew him in Spring Falls. Strangely enough, it was why it was dangerous for him to be here. Because he was a stranger in town, someone might ask about him only because they didn't know who he was. But Harry was counting on the fact that people rarely noticed old men. Because this time, what needed to be done could only be done by him.

Why he had waited this long to deal with the past was hard to say. Probably because, despite his reputation as a predator when it came to business dealings, Harry knew he was a coward in life.

He had lived his whole life behind the scenes, pulling strings, making things happen, watching like a hawk over people's lives. And then doing what was necessary for whatever he considered the greater good. But uncharacteristically, although he had carefully watched over the life of someone in this room, he had done nothing to hurt or help.

Harry knew that staying away, and doing nothing, had been a cowardly thing to do. It was so much easier to observe from a distance. It was safe living inside a world that he created and controlled. However, his doctor's diagnosis confirmed what he already knew. Which meant it was time to do something that he should have done years before.

As the red-haired woman and her friends began moving through the crowd, Harry turned, and leaning heavily on his cane, walked quietly out the front door, and into the frigid air.

The winter wind snapped through the trees, bringing with it the smell of smoke that he could see streaming from one of the houses down the street. He had always loved that smell, and Harry wondered why he hadn't indulged himself more often with a fire in the winter.

A car door opened, Harry ducked his head, threw his cane in first, and then folded himself into the back seat. As the car moved away from the Ruby House and into the night, Harry turned and looked back at the crowd streaming out the front door. He caught a glimpse of her as she stood in the doorway, saying goodbye to the crowd.

Yes, he had some wrongs to make right, but timing was everything, and today was not the day.

Two

Marsha Melinda Martin lay on her back in the middle of the floor on her rose-colored yoga mat in the big downstairs room of the Ruby House and stared at the newly painted ceiling. She closed her eyes and opened them again. No, nothing had changed. She was still lying on the floor, wishing she was someone who had courage and vision and could just decide to do something and then do it.

Instead, she waited for the right timing for almost everything, which was pretty much never. The reason she had gotten as much done as she had in April's house was because everyone kept pushing her to complete the project, and even more so because she wanted April to come home.

As Marsha lay on her mat, she watched the early morning light stream through the curtainless windows filtered through the maple tree outside the window. The red haze from the buds made patterns on the floor that looked like a dance to Marsha.

Once a dancer alway a dancer, she thought. *Even when you don't act like one,* she added. But the yoga mat was part of her recently formed determination to renovate herself the same way she and Seth were renovating the house.

Seth was the foreman, Judith handled the money, and Marsha made sure everything flowed well. This was all with April's permission, who promised that she would return when she was ready.

But it had been months now, and April still wasn't home. They had fixed the plumbing, updated the electricity, patched cracks in the walls, painted, and replaced the roof—and still no April.

They had recorded everything, hoping that when April returned, she could use the videos to start her design business. And now that they were done with all the repairs, and April still hadn't returned to Spring Falls—instead of finding something else to do, Marsha lay on the gleaming wooden floor and asked herself why she seemed incapable of deciding anything or moving on.

Even though almost a year had gone by since she had returned to Spring Falls, she was still living at Cindy's house. During that time, Bree had found the daughter she thought she had lost. Mary was living in Spring Falls with her husband Seth and their new baby girl, Rho. Judith and Bruce were falling in love. And April had discovered that her husband of over thirty years was a serial killer. Big, big changes.

But she and Cindy were as they were before. Cindy was running her art gallery, while trying to hide the fact that she was painting again, and Marsha was lying on the floor of the Ruby House trying to hide her terror at becoming part of the world and doing something with her life.

Fixing the Ruby House had been easy for her to do because it was a project with a purpose, and she could hide behind the scenes while doing it. She had thrown herself into the project until now. Now it was ready for April's touch, and she felt lost again.

April, Marsha sighed, thinking of her friend who had gone so far away. April had left Spring Falls to be with her children as they absorbed what they learned about their father. It was the right thing to do, but Marsha missed her so much that sometimes it felt as if her heart was living in Canada with April.

It surprised her. Marsha had thought of herself as a loyal friend, always supportive, but definitely not someone who would miss anyone when they weren't there.

After all, she had left Spring Falls and moved to New York to dance on Broadway without a second glance back at her friends. Sure, she had kept in touch once in a while. She had let them know when she moved out of New York to open a dance studio once she discovered she would never be good enough to be a Broadway star.

But, if Bree's husband had not sent them all a letter asking them to take care of Bree after he passed away, she might not have ever seen her friends again. So missing people was not her style at all. Or at least she hadn't known it until now.

Sitting up, Marsha stared at herself in the row of mirrors that lined one wall of what was going to be a dance studio. What she saw was a woman who had gained a little too much weight, whose hair had been dyed a little too blond, wearing clothes a little too tight and much too old to be considered fashionable.

What has happened to me? Marsha asked herself. *And are you going to do anything about it?*

Her cell phone lying beside her vibrated. It was a message from Judith.

Of course it's Judith, Marsha mumbled to herself. Judith was relentless. *It is almost as if she can see me lying here doing nothing.*

"Let's have a business meeting," Judith texted.

Sighing, Marsha answered, "yes," as she unconsciously moved through a down-dog to get herself off the floor.

"Lunch at ParaTi's in an hour?" Judith asked.

"Okay," Marsha responded, and sighed again to herself. She knew why Judith chose a public place. It was so Marsha would have to make herself look presentable.

She both hated and loved Judith for her consistent pressure to be doing something, being someone.

Easy for you, Judith, Marsha said to herself, knowing she was whining again. She could blame all her problems on her terrible childhood with a drunk mother and a nonexistent father. But lots of people had terrible childhoods and managed their lives just fine.

"It's the secrets you keep that make it worse, and that's your fault," Marsha said to the woman in the mirror.

Maybe I should get Mimi and Janet to make me over, Marsha thought, thinking back to the changes the two of them had made in April when she moved back to Spring Falls.

Marsha looked around the room, seeing herself once more in the mirror as she did so. Behind her, she could see the silhouette of the tree reaching for the light. Trees remade themselves every year. Why couldn't she? The overweight, unkempt woman in the mirror couldn't be her. She used to be so much more.

Marsha knew she did nothing about herself because she was a coward. And she was starting to hate being a coward. Eventually, her sense of adventure would have to kick in. She knew it would. It had happened before. Otherwise, how had she gotten herself to New York?

But, Marsha had to admit, this time she might need a big push to get going. She hoped it would be a gentle push, but maybe that was too much to ask for.

Three

Judith placed her cell phone on the desk in her office, adjusted the small plaque on her desk that said, "Judith Zoe Accountant," and stared at the closed door. She knew there were clients waiting on the other side. Her assistant, Nancy, had buzzed her more than once to remind her she was running behind schedule.

Judith liked her office, maybe even loved it. It was her space, and like all her spaces, it was arranged just the way she wanted it to be. Her leather and chrome chair fit her perfectly, and if she swiveled just a bit, she could see the pictures she had so carefully chosen to impart comfort and strength and perhaps a little inspiration.

She had the walls painted a soft pink that was so light that people often thought they were off-white. Judith, with April's help, had chosen pink on purpose. It calmed and soothed. Plus, it set off her coloring. Judith wasn't vain. She was practical. She was in the business of fixing things, putting things in order, and assuring her clients that all would be well. Everything helped.

Including the light scent from the fresh flowers that always sat on top of the wood cabinet to her right. The long low cabinet that contained all her files, files that were never laid out where they would clutter the space and her mind. To her clients, Judith looked as if she always had everything in control, and that was exactly how she liked it.

There was a window behind her that looked out into an alley, so Judith wasn't missing the view by being in front of it. She had placed a light film covering on the window so that no one could see in. Gauzy white curtains floated in front of it, adding to the sense of lightness and comfort she wanted her clients to feel.

And, yes, Judith had placed her desk in front of the window on purpose. The light from the covered window wasn't so bright that it blinded her clients, but it hid her face and revealed theirs. It was how she always met new clients. If it was someone she knew well, she lowered a blind behind the curtains and flicked on the lights embedded in the ceiling above the window so they could all see each other equally.

The clients waiting for her were people she knew well, so she had lowered the blind and turned on the lights. Everything was in place, but still Judith waited. She leaned back in her chair, fingers steepled, thinking about April and Ron and what she could have done better, and what she could do now.

Although the Town Meeting she had held months before had gone well, some people in town were still gossiping about the horror show that Ron Page had been. And even though they should know better, many people wondered how his wife of over thirty years had not known.

The question is, how did none of us know? Judith asked herself. If April was to blame, they all were. But they hadn't known. And to blame themselves, or anyone but Ron, was both foolish and dangerous because it kept them locked into anger, guilt, and sorrow, and they needed to move forward.

Judith had told them all to let the police continue their search for Ron, but they would rebuild their lives and the town based on the principles Judith so firmly believed in. Community kindness and community action. They didn't have to agree with each other about everything, but they did need to respect and listen to each other.

It was how she had built her business, and the result was she had her hand in almost every business in town. Which made her the perfect pivot person for the town's rebirth out of the Ron Page, serial-killer-at-large story.

Judith huffed at herself for even thinking of Ron. She had people to take care of, and she had a plan for at least one of her friends. Like it or not, she was going to make sure they all not only survived, but thrived, despite what they had gone through.

As always, her thoughts moved first to April. When April and Ron had moved away after college, she and April had kept up weekly phone calls. And now that April was in Canada with her daughter and her family, Judith had started up the weekly calls again. But just as it had been when April lived in Silver Lake, they only brushed the surface of what was going on in April's life.

Judith understood April didn't feel ready to talk too deeply about what had happened. April's first concern was her children, and that was how it should be. Still, Judith knew that eventually, April would have to return to Spring Falls and rebuild her life. It was her home now. April had a dream called the Ruby House, and Judith knew she couldn't let April forget about that dream. She just had to give her time.

But there was another person who needed her direct attention. Marsha. Marsha was a pro at avoiding her, even though they worked together on the house. And to make sure they stayed in touch, Judith hosted Ruby Sister gatherings at her house at least every two weeks. And still Marsha felt almost as distant as April.

They always invited April to join them during their gatherings using Zoom. Sometimes she popped in for a minute, barely lit on the screen, hiding herself. Their light-hearted wren no longer laughed at everything, or found delight in the simple pleasure of getting together.

When April hung up, the rest of them would talk about what Mimi and Janet had named their project: Bring April Back. But most of it was just a matter of being patient and waiting while being available for whatever April needed.

Mostly time, Judith reminded herself. But Marsha was another story. She was present in Spring Falls and yet she wasn't. And being Judith, she would have to find out what was going on with her.

Judith picked up her cell and asked Marsha to lunch. Yes, she'd find out what was behind Marsha's reluctance to move on. She would get her to share what was bothering Marsha. Because, like April's return, finding out Marsha's secret was inevitable.

Putting the phone back on her desk and smiling to herself, Judith leaned forward, pushed the button on her desk and said to Nancy, "I'm ready."

Four

The subject of Marsha and Judith's thoughts was still in bed. Her daughter, Amanda, had installed her in their small spare bedroom. It was supposed to be the babies' room, so it had a changing table, cartoon figures on the walls, deep blue painted walls, and stick-on stars covered the ceiling. It felt appropriate to April. Her life was starting over, just like a baby. Except she wasn't so innocent.

April was sleeping on a pull-out couch that Amanda and her husband, John, had kept in the room from before it became the babies' room. It had been handy for short-term visitors. When April first arrived, the bearer of news no one wanted to hear, April knew they believed she would be a short-term visitor. That she had been here for months was not what they had counted on. And she knew they didn't like it.

Before buying the couch, Amanda and her husband John had obviously not pulled the bed out to see how flimsy the mattress was. April could almost feel the springs underneath, and she sometimes lay on a blanket to pad the mattress so her bones didn't feel bruised in the morning.

Not that she would tell her daughter about it. April did her best to stay out of Amanda's and John's way. They were still reeling from the news she had brought them. That, coupled with the birth of their son soon after she arrived, left them emotionally and physically exhausted.

The boy, Noah, was supposed to be sleeping in this room. They had perfectly planned everything until April showed up, turning their world upside down. Now Noah slept in their bedroom instead. April could hear him crying in the night, and she knew he kept both his parents awake because it kept her awake and she was one room away.

She couldn't sleep anyway, so she kept telling them to put the baby in with her, but they refused. Her daughter, stubborn as always, was also angry. Angry at April for showing up with devastating news. Angry at April for having a husband like Ron, who ended up being her father. Angry that she hadn't known. Angry that although at first she and April had cried together, now April was a constant reminder that Amanda's life with loving parents had all been a lie.

Amanda had thought her father was just one of those distant men, like some of her friends' fathers. Men who were distant because they were busy building a business. Yes, her father was busy building a business. But he was doing much more than that. He was also busy killing women.

April knew that Amanda's husband was also angry. He was asking himself, what kind of family had he married into? And despite the lack of logic involved, she knew John worried his son would grow up to be like his grandfather, Ron.

As April lay in bed, she could hear her daughter and her husband whispering about what to do. This was what they often did. Whispered when she wasn't around. But at the same time, April knew, and they knew, that she heard them anyway.

Amanda and John talked about moving out of Canada and not revealing where they were going. Not even to April, in case she would tell Ron. As if she would. Already wounded by Ron, each time her daughter looked at her with distrust, another dagger plunged through her heart.

Her son, Robert, having been summoned by April to come to Amanda's house so they could talk, stayed only one day. Long enough to say he had always distrusted his father and now he knew why, and thank god they hadn't named him Ron Jr.

Robert had let himself sob for a moment on April's shoulder and ask her if it meant he would be like his father, and then, sitting up, said he was leaving again.

"Where will you go?" April asked, hoping at least one of her children would understand that she needed them. His answer was he didn't know. He was going to look into changing his name and then continue to travel. That various companies employed him as a travel writer gave him the freedom to do what he wanted.

April wanted to tell Robert that he could never be like his father, that he was like her father, warm and carefree. But she didn't have the chance. The next morning there was a note on the kitchen table saying he was sorry, but he had to leave.

April knew Robert had a boyfriend. He had at least shared that much. April prayed he was someone Robert could count on, and that someday Robert would find her and be her son again.

But her daughter was a different story. And yet here April was months later, still living in her daughter's house, feeling the resentment seeping into everything that she did and said. Instead of finding comfort, or bringing comfort, she had brought pain. April not only felt unwanted, but sometimes hated. Could she blame Amanda and John for their dislike of her? She couldn't. It was all her fault.

The only light in April's life was Noah. She loved rocking him while Amanda and John were busy, or when he wouldn't stop crying. Holding him, she calmed him and herself down, humming so quietly no one could hear her, but Noah felt it.

Holding Noah was the only time she felt as if his parents were glad that she was in their house. And little Noah didn't care about all the things she had done wrong, or about the past. He would lift his blue eyes up to her, give her a wobbly grin, and lay his head back down on her chest, and fall asleep.

If no one was looking, April would cry, covering Noah with her hand so that her tears wouldn't drop onto his head. Leaning back in the rocker, she asked herself over and over again how she had not known.

At night she relived throwing herself out of the car, trying to escape the horror that her life had turned into. In the day, she relived each moment of her life, and how she had turned a blind eye to what was now clear.

April had hoped that if she stayed long enough, Amanda's resentment and anger would fade. But if anything, it had gotten worse. It was time to leave. She knew it was, even though she didn't want to and had no idea where she could go.

But April knew it was time. Not only was she making her daughter and husband miserable, she was afraid that she was putting them in danger. She knew Ron would never bother with his children, because he had never bothered with them when he was trying to act like a father. But he might come for her.

Now she knew Ron considered her his property, and he believed she was the only person he ever loved. He had told her, there in the car, while he told her about his secret life. Thinking back to that moment, April sobbed, hiding under the covers in the bed. Ron knew nothing about love.

Booker had kept April updated with what law enforcement was doing. The search was still on, but they had lost his trail. The last thing they had on him was his transferring money to a bank in Canada. But that money had disappeared along with him.

Booker had assured her they would find him, but April knew they were waiting for him to make a mistake. And knowing Ron, that might never happen. Instead, he'd find a way to get to her with no one knowing. If that was what he wanted to do. April hoped it wasn't. But April's belief in hope had faded the moment Ron had told her his secret.

Yes, April knew it was time to leave. But where could she go? Judith and the Ruby Sisters kept begging her to come home. But could she? Could she go back to the town where everyone knew her? Maybe she should run away like her son did. That would keep all of them safe.

However, at that moment, all she wanted to do was stay in bed, pull the covers up over her head, and pray to all the gods she ever heard of that all of this had only been a dream.

Five

April stayed in bed, staying out of the way, knowing how delighted Amanda and John would be not to have her at the breakfast table. She listened to the sounds of the house, the creaking of the heater as it came on. She could hear Amanda speaking softly to Noah as she fed him, John showering, dressing, and then the door shutting behind him as he left for work.

Memories showed up like movies in her head. She couldn't stop them even if she wanted to. Clear and bright. She saw herself when Amanda was Noah's age. The house was quiet and peaceful after Ron had left for work.

Robert would play quietly at her feet as she rocked Amanda. He'd tell her stories about what land he was building using the hundreds of Legos that cluttered the floor until they all ended up as castles and trees and faraway places. Even then, Robert was dreaming of seeing things she would never see.

As Robert talked, she'd encourage his imagination with questions. Then she would look down at her precious Amanda lying in her arms, long lashes resting on her cheeks, and think she had the best life in the world. Amanda sleeping in her arms, Robert smiling up at her as he built his kingdom, contentment enveloping them all.

How had she not seen then that the moment Ron walked in the door, all that peace and contentment would be replaced with a frisson of tension, the need to mold herself to him taking over? All those years and she had not known.

April screamed inside her head, covering her ears as if that would stop the sound. She had ruined her children's lives because of her ignorance. And now they hated her. And they should. It was all her fault.

More hours passed. Amanda knocked on her door asking if she was alright. Her mumbled "yes" seemed to satisfy her daughter, and April rolled over and wished she had died when she jumped out of the car.

But you didn't, she said to herself. *So now what? You can't keep making Amanda's and John's life miserable. You need to make a new life now.*

Those words didn't come from the screaming voice in her head, but from somewhere deep inside her. Instead of a fire of emotions that the screaming voice brought, these words felt as light as butterfly wings. They moved softly inside the sorrow and rage that had enveloped her for months, and she felt some of those emotions slide away.

April sat up, threw off the covers, and stumbled to the bathroom. *Enough of feeling sorry for myself,* she said out loud.

As she showered, April thought back to a conversation she had with Bree one morning. Just the two of them. Bree had shared how when the sorrow and pain of missing her husband overcame her, she would imagine herself as something other than Bree, the woman who gave her daughter up for adoption and lost her husband.

She'd imagine herself as a person she admired, or an animal, depending on what she needed. Bree told her that sometimes she imagined herself as April, the light-hearted, carefree wren that she had been when they first met and throughout high school.

The thought made April cry, her tears mixing with water from the shower. Bree—who had never told her it was her husband Ron who had raped her, and was the father of her child—still loved April and imagined herself to be her when she needed comfort.

Well, if Bree could do that, I can do it too, April said to herself. *I'll imagine myself as a woman who knows what to do and how to do it. I will imagine myself in a new life, one I made myself. I'll imagine myself as strong and courageous.*

And then, glimpsing herself as she stepped out of the shower, she laughed. She'd have to have a good imagination. Because right now she looked as wispy as the moth that kept circling her night light. Barely there. No sign of the bright, happy wren that Bree believed her to be.

But all that would change. She'd pull herself together and get on with it. *I'm a lioness,* April said to herself. It was such a ridiculous thought that April giggled.

It was the first time she had even smiled in months. That was one step forward.

An hour later, April was dressed, packed, and bumping her suitcase down the staircase. She had taken the sheets off the couch and closed it. She had made the spare bedroom as neat as she could. Standing inside the small room, she envisioned Noah and her daughter rocking together and smiled inside. Her heart broke. But she knew that leaving was the best thing she could do for them.

Amanda came out of the kitchen as April rolled the suitcase to the front door.

"Mom? Where are you going?"

"Not sure yet, but it's time to move on."

"Mom," Amanda cried. And at that moment, April knew that although her daughter was mad at her, and disappointed, she also loved her. And if April could rebuild her life, they might have a future together.

Stepping forward, she gathered Amanda in her arms and let all the love she felt for her surround them both.

"Don't worry, sweetie. I'll be okay. I promise to let you know where I am. But it's time for everyone to move on. Thank you for giving me a place to stay these past few months."

Releasing Amanda from the hug, she grabbed both her hands. The two of them stood together as the tears flowed. April looked up at her beautiful daughter and smiled at her through the tears.

"I am so proud of you, Amanda. You and your brother. I couldn't ask for more. Now, I need to become someone you two can be proud of, too. Will you hug Noah and tell him I'll see him soon? And John. A good man.

"I love you, Amanda," April said as she opened the front door and stepped outside.

The car she had ordered had pulled up to the curb. Having flown to her daughter's house, the first thing she needed to do was buy a car.

Then decide where to go from there. Because April was sure about one thing. She was not yet ready to return to Spring Falls. She had to find herself first.

Six

It had taken Bruce Dawson a few months to complete his move to Spring Falls. His old house sold almost immediately. But the new owner couldn't move in for a few months, so they had arranged where Bruce could stay to complete the transfer of his clients over to the husband and wife team who had purchased his estate planning business.

The transfer had gone as smoothly as he had hoped it would. His assistant stayed on with the new owners, and he gave her a bonus as a thank you for all that she did to keep things going so well.

He had met with each client personally and explained the transfer to the new owners. After meeting them, most of his clients were happy. Only a few took their business elsewhere. And even a few said they'd make the two-hour drive to his new office in Spring Falls to keep him as their attorney.

Bruce was not entirely sure they would do that once time had gone by, but he was happy to keep them on. What had surprised and touched him was that every client wished him luck in his new venture.

While making the decision to move, Bruce decided he wanted to work from home. Which turned out to be possible in Spring Falls. So he had purchased a house a few blocks from the center of town, and hired Mary's husband Seth to help him renovate it.

Because it had to be done first so he could continue to work only the office was done so far. Bruce didn't care how long it took to make his home look good. He knew he had made the right decision. Every day, he was happier than he thought it was possible to be.

Judith lived within walking distance. He could walk into town for coffee or food, or visit Cindy, Mimi, and Janet at the art gallery. Once the weather got better, he planned to explore the trails that led into the surrounding forests and farmland.

On one almost spring day, Bree had taken him on the trail to the falls that they had named the town for. It had rained a few days before and the falls were fuller than they had been for a while, so they heard it long before they reached it.

As they sat on a bench near the falls, both of them wrapped up in winter coats and hats, drops from the falls glinting in the sunlight on their coats, they had talked that day about all the changes they had all gone through in the past year. Bree was still grieving her husband Paul's death, but was grateful that she now had a family that she thought she had lost. Plus, she was spending time with Booker, her high-school boyfriend.

Bree told Bruce that she and Booker were taking it slow. Even though Paul had obviously set it all up that she would return to Spring Falls with the Ruby Sisters, find her daughter, and perhaps rekindling her romance with Booker, she wanted to do it in her own timing.

"Paul was a remarkable man, wasn't he?" Bruce said, and Bree had dropped her head onto Bruce's shoulder and agreed, trying not to cry over what could never be again.

And even though they both knew that Paul had moved on, they still took a moment and thanked him once again for his last gift. Because Bruce knew Paul had also thought that he and Judith would like each other. And they did. Surprising and delighting them both.

But today, Bruce was preparing for his first new client in Spring Falls. He stood in his upstairs bedroom and tried not to notice all that needed to be done. Instead, he focused on the view outside his window.

He missed the apple tree that was outside his old office window, but his tiny backyard already showed promise. Instead of an apple tree, a red-bud stood ready to bloom. And when the landscaper that Seth recommended stopped by to access the garden, he told Bruce there were many mature plants there, and it would be easy to turn it into a blooming paradise. Bruce couldn't wait to get started. Just a few more weeks and the ground would be ready.

Turning to the mirrored closet doors, Bruce straightened his tie, checked to make sure his sandy gray hair was in place and that he had nothing in his teeth, and headed downstairs to the office.

For the time being, Judith's assistant, Nancy, was also taking his phone calls and setting up appointments for him. Once his practice became busier he'd hire someone, but for now, it worked for both of them. It was easy to re-direct the calls to Nancy. She just had to remember that one line was for Judith and one was for him.

"Why don't you put your two practices in the same building?" she had asked them when they had asked for her help. Both of them shook their heads no.

"We like it this way," was Judith's answer, and Bruce agreed. They didn't have to spend every minute of the day together to enjoy their new relationship. Both of them were much too independent anyway, and they were negotiating how to be in a relationship and stay that way. "Not like other people," they would say to each other once in a while.

Sitting in his office chair, Bruce looked over his office. It wasn't like Judith's. There were windows that looked out onto the street and heavy curtains he could close at night if he wanted to. He had his desk and chair from his old office, a few comfortable chairs for clients, and not much else. He wanted to live in it for a while before making any major changes.

On his desk was the iPad he used for making notes. Later he'd add the notes to his computer, but talking face to face with clients, he wanted them to feel safe and cared for, and a computer just got in the way.

Estate planning was hard for most people. They were planning for loved ones, knowing that someday they wouldn't be there for them. Some of them found it a straightforward thing to do. Putting their affairs in order gave them pleasure. Others dreaded it, and he had a box of tissues on his desk always ready for the ones that broke down.

Bruce wondered what this client wanted. He'd never heard of him, and did not know why he had come to him. For a moment, Bruce wondered if this new client would change his life as much as Paul Mann had when he had come to him to plan his estate. Or would it be a simple thing for everyone involved?

But Bruce's intuition told him it would be the former. Whoever this Harry Harrison was, it was going to be a life changer for someone. Maybe even him.

Seven

"Where is she going?" Cindy asked Judith.

They were together at their favorite coffee shop, holding their regular Monday morning meeting, the one they kept no matter what else was going on. They had started the tradition when they were the only two Ruby Sisters who had stayed in Spring Falls.

Over the years, the coffee shop had changed. The major change happened when a franchise coffee shop opened in Spring Falls. Judith had convinced them it was inevitable other coffee shops would follow. Their choices were to either reinvent themselves, sell, or close the shop.

They chose transformation—to become a unique and cozy destination. They paneled the ceiling, changed the lighting, put in electrical outlets for computers, and painted the walls. Then they changed their focus to specialty coffees, baked some of their own pastries and bought others from local suppliers. They ground their own beans which scented the air, often drawing people in off of the street heading down to the franchise shop.

The changes had made them a popular place to be. There was always a mix of town-folk and college kids in the shop. Although at this time of the morning, on a Monday, it was fairly empty, a few people sitting alone typing away on their computers. Judith thought they either were looking for a quiet space to work, or they loved having people around them as white noise.

Cindy and Judith had their favorite table in the back of the shop where their talking could not be overheard. In the summer, they often sat outside, but it wasn't warm enough yet. Besides, rain was in the forecast and wind from the northwest was bringing it.

At the moment, Cindy and Judith were sharing an enormous elephant-ear pastry. It was perfect. Flaky, crunchy, with the perfect blend of butter and sugar. A woman who ran a small bakery just outside of town provided them to the coffee shop. Of course, Judith was the baker's accountant, and made sure that even though it was small, it was profitable and well run.

Licking the crumbs off her fingers, Judith answered Cindy's question about April. "She doesn't know. All she told me was that she knew she wasn't ready to come back here. Yet."

It was the "yet" that cheered them both. They needed April to come home so they could be part of her healing. And theirs. They all suffered from what Ron had done. But of course, it was April's life that had been turned upside down.

However, although Judith and Cindy understood why April couldn't come home yet, it still hurt. Neither one of them had to say it out loud. *Especially Judith*, Cindy thought. *She'd just soldier on, making things work, fixing whatever she could when she could.*

Sighing, Cindy ate the last bit of her pastry, savoring it, wanting more, and knowing she'd have to wait until next week. If she stuck to her good habits, maybe she could get rid of her bad ones.

Cindy wanted to be a better friend and fully accept why April couldn't come home, but she was stuck between that and needing

April to return so she could focus on helping her. It would take her mind off her own life.

Sipping her coffee, Cindy tried to be grateful. After all, putting the Ron and April story aside, she was happy. Mostly. The problem was, she wasn't sure at all about herself anymore. And she used to be sure, or she thought she had been. Now, her sometimes confused state of mind about whether or not she was an artist made her question everything.

Of course, Cindy knew her problems did not compare to a woman finding out her long-time husband was a serial rapist and killer. *How do you live with that?* Cindy thought. And then sent a silent prayer to April, hoping it helped.

"How did she buy a car? Does she have enough money?"

"Remember when you convinced her to open her own checking account in town?"

Cindy nodded.

"Well. When Ron bought her that house, he paid for it completely, and put it in her name only. He also gave her money to renovate it, and she put that into her new checking account. All of it in her name only. And when she and Marsha decided to work together, she transferred some of it into another account, just for the house, so Marsha would have access to it.

"Plus, get this. Ron told her when he bought the house that he had a savings account that he had been putting money into it for her and the children for years. When he bought the house, he told her about it. So money is not April's problem."

"So, I guess Ron loved April?"

"I think he did. Does probably. But maybe all of that money giving made him feel important. You know how much he liked to be admired for how much money he made in his business. That's shut down, of course. But I am sure he isn't hurting for money either. If he took care of April that way, he surely did that for himself."

"It sounds as if he was always preparing for the moment he would have to disappear."

"It does. Although I doubt he believed he would ever be caught. But it was—well is—his nature to be prepared. Which means it's doubtful they will ever find him."

Both of them paused for a moment, wondering if that was a good thing or bad thing for April. Because, for them, April had to come first.

"So she has everything she needs, and she promised to keep in touch?"

"Yes. I have power of attorney over her accounts, in case I need to get extra funds for her. And she promised to keep that app on her phone, that we all have, that tracks where she goes. She also promised to show up on Zoom for our Ruby Sister meetings when she can."

Cindy sighed, thinking that would have to be good enough. But if April didn't come home soon, maybe she would go get her the same way she had gone to get Bree when her husband died.

"One more thing," Judith said. "She asked me if she can divorce Ron even if she can't find him. And in the meantime, she wants to legally change her name back to her maiden name. Not my specialty, but I have a friend who will help her with that."

"If she could get a divorce, won't that make Ron mad at her? Wouldn't that be dangerous? That love for her could turn into hatred instead and then he might come after her," Cindy said, thinking about how horrible that would be.

"Possible. Right now though, she is no longer April Page to us. She is as she was when we all met, April May Zane."

Cindy smiled, and Judith glanced out the window, remembering how she had first met April. They were in line in second grade. The two Z's at the back of the line. And how their meeting had changed them both forever.

That bond would never fade. She'd make sure of that.

Eight

Bree knew that Cindy and Judith were having their regular Monday morning coffee meeting. Just the two of them. Usually, she didn't care. After all, she had her morning routine, and it did not include being social in a coffee shop.

But today, she wished she had that excuse to get out of the house. Away from the computer and the writing that wasn't going well. Well, nothing was going well. A few days earlier, the keys on the computer she used to write were doing strange things, and she had to spend hours figuring out what had gone wrong.

Then yesterday her phone died, forcing her to the local phone store where, despite telling herself she wouldn't do it, she had upgraded her phone and bought all the accessories necessary at the store, even though she knew they were overpriced.

Although the salespeople at the store were very helpful, and got everything working for her, (they were sales people after all), she still found herself resentful of having to spend all that money when all she wanted was her phone to work.

It took hours out of her day. Despite that, some things on her phone still didn't work the same. Yes, it was a better phone. *Yes,* she said to herself, *I do like it better*. Still, she was caught up in the resentment that she had to change everything and that so many companies still choose profit first.

How rude, she said out loud to herself, as she stood at the glass door in her kitchen that led out into the patio she had Seth lay for her last summer. Well, he actually didn't. He found someone and supervised it.

The "how rude" statement made her laugh at herself. Bree knew she often said that when things didn't go exactly her way. She had said the same thing about the problems with the patio's cost and the effort it took to make it happen. And now she loved it.

If it wasn't blowing a small gale outside, she'd take her coffee outside and feel sorry for herself out there. Instead, what she was supposed to be doing was sitting at her computer writing the book she had started so many months before.

She had been so sure of the story. Happy to be writing a new book in her own name. It had started out well, then stalled when they discovered what Ron had been doing. And stalled more because she had to tell Mary the truth about Ron being her father. Bree thought Mary took the news better than she handled the telling. But she had worked through that and came back to the writing. It was going fairly well, except now she was halfway through the book and found she hated it.

Of course she did. All the writers she knew hated the book that they were working on halfway through the book. What she had learned to do was to keep writing anyway. Another twenty chapters and the book would resolve itself and the ending would reveal what even she hadn't thought would happen.

But it had never taken her this long to write a book before. When she wasn't busy being upset with herself for not getting things done, she understood why. All the adventures, the sadness, the despair, the terror, the telling of her long-held secret, and even the joy of finding her daughter and holding her new grandchild were all stressful and major distractions.

Give yourself a break, Bree said to herself.

What she meant was to stop being so hard on herself, but then she realized that giving herself a break was probably also a good idea. A break, meaning doing something different. Maybe a trip somewhere.

Bree knew that her best ideas happened when she was out walking, or cooking something, when her mind was busy with something else letting the creative muse in. She'd rush to her iPad, or a piece of paper, and write out the idea before it moved on. Claiming it for herself.

She, like many creatives, believed that ideas flowed freely through the universe and when someone didn't pick it and do something with it, it moved on to the next person. So if she didn't keep them quickly, and then do something with them, the idea flowed to the next person who would.

Of course, she couldn't keep all the ideas that came to her. Some just passed through, claiming her attention for a moment. And then, after examining it to see if it fit her, if it didn't, she'd let it go.

But lately, those ideas had not flowed in. Or if they had, she had not heard them. A trip would open up space for them.

I could go now, Bree thought. *Grab a few clothes, get my computer, new phone, and just start driving. Somewhere. Out of town.* There was a garden near Philadelphia she had always wanted to see. Not that far away. She'd make it in less than a day.

All she had to do was text her daughter, and all the Ruby Sisters, that she would be gone for a week or so. And then leave before anyone tried to change her mind.

No, she thought. *I'll leave and then text. That way, no one can talk me out of it.*

Although she often babysat for granddaughter Rho, when her daughter Mary worked and Seth was busy, she knew all the other Ruby Sisters would gladly step in. Plus, Mary was a capable young woman with friends of her own. *Yes. Everyone will be fine without me*, Bree thought.

What about Booker, she reminded herself. She had a tentative lunch date scheduled with him on Wednesday. *I'll text him, too,* she said to herself. *Once I am out of town.*

He'd understand. He was often canceling their "dates" due to work. Although at first she was afraid of reestablishing her relationship with him, now she enjoyed it because it had settled into a friendship, but not a romance. And that was more than fine with her.

Paul was her one and only, and she loved being on her own. Because just as she was going to do right now, she made her own life just the way she wanted to. Decided her own schedule. Yes, she loved living on her own. And choosing to go when she wanted to, where she wanted to.

And she loved having her friends that were always there for each other. She had the best of both worlds this way. Friends and freedom.

Glancing at the clock on the kitchen wall, she told herself she could be out of the house within an hour. Before she left, she needed to put the trash out, make sure that the dishes were clean, and everything was neat and tidy. She'd hate coming back from a trip to find a mess.

Pack and go. Tell people later.

Excitement coursed through her as she raced around, doing all the little things that needed to be done. Yes, this was exactly what she needed.

Nine

The lunch with Judith on Friday had simultaneously helped Marsha and pissed her off. Which, strangely, was also helpful. And Marsha knew that Judith, the supreme mover and shaker, had known and didn't care.

Because Judith knew that even while Marsha was angry, she understood that Judith's intent was to help, and sometimes she had to make people angry for that to happen. In that way, Judith and Bree were the same. The need to be liked was not their driving force.

Which also pissed Marsha off. Because when she was telling herself the truth, which she often did even though just as often she ignored it, Marsha knew that being liked was important to her. And no matter how much she didn't want that to be true, there it was, sticking out like a big sore toe. Every time she thought someone didn't like her or simply didn't care about her, she stubbed that toe again.

So now, days later, she was back at the Ruby House, once again sitting on the floor on her yoga mat. But instead of wishing she knew what to do—after her annoying lunch with Judith, and a weekend of thinking about it—she thought she would know. But would she? That remained to be seen.

She needed someone to talk to about it. She could have talked to Cindy because Cindy loved being helpful. Not in a Judith sort of way, but in an I-want-to-be-helpful-because-it feels-so-good-to-me kind of way. So Cindy might be able to help, if she let her.

But she had lived in Cindy's house for almost a year now, which made her feel guilty thinking what a parasite she had been. So Marsha worried about giving Cindy the opportunity to help. *Which is really messed up*, Marsha thought.

The person she really needed to talk to was April. April who had abandoned her. *Which was a completely selfish thing to think*. But there it was, and she was trying to be truthful, at least to herself.

And the truth was, she had to tell April something. Something she should have told her when Ron's hidden life was uncovered. But, coward that she was, she didn't. And now Marsha felt even more alone than she ever had, and it was her own fault.

But besides what she had to tell April, she also had to ask her permission to go forward with building the dance-theatre-arts center that would take up the entire first floor of the Ruby House. It had been the plan before the Ron reveal, so Marsha was fairly sure that Judith was right—as always—that April would tell her to go ahead with it.

But Marsha hated the idea of developing the center. She wanted a partner, a friend, to do it with her. And not just any friend or partner. She wanted April.

But there were too many problems attached to that wanting. Marsha knew she had to let it go. Had to stop wanting what she couldn't have. Stop wishing she wasn't who she was and was someone else. Someone like Judith or Bree, who always seemed so sure of themselves.

She had to stop delaying and waiting for the right moment. As if there was a right moment. She had to stop feeling alone when she wasn't. Judith had suggested counseling. Maybe she should do that. But then someone besides her would know the secret.

That's the point, you idiot, she said to herself. *That's why you get counseling, so someone else knows and helps you work through it.*

Just thinking about it made Marsha want to eat as much chocolate as she could find as fast as she could. *At least I am only a food addict, not a drug addic*t, she said to herself. Knowing that the word addict didn't care what kind you were, it was that you were. And that required getting some kind of help.

But like all her secrets, Marsha had told no one, not able to face the feelings she had that despite being surrounded by friends who intellectually she knew loved her, she still felt unloved. And felt as if she deserved to be alone.

Imagining a conversation with her mother, she asked her why she had never told her about her father. Why had she drunk herself to death? Did he leave because she was an alcoholic, or did she become one after he left? Did he know she existed? Did he leave before or after she was born?

All these secrets her mother kept from her. She had asked a few times but had been told it wasn't important. How could it not be important? How she hated the secrets her mother had kept from her.

And now she was just like her mother—keeping secrets. Would she ever get the courage to tell them? Had she blown them up into something more important than they actually were just because she hadn't told?

Marsha stood, and as she had every day for months, stared at herself in the mirror and asked herself if she could do it. Could she lose the weight and find the courage to live as the person she wanted to be? She had done it before. Although briefly. Dance and theatre had saved her. Could they do it again? Could she let go of the stories that lived in her head about being unwanted and live as someone else?

When she had danced, the music would carry her away. Theatre brought her into another world. Sometimes it was a painful world, but she was always aware it was just a story. Not truth. Not her life.

In her head she heard Bree say to her, but what if all of life is a story? Marsha watched in the mirror as tears ran down her face at the thought. If it was true, then perhaps she could rewrite her story.

And you could help others to rewrite their story through what you and April want to do here, Marsha said to herself. *If you do it for someone else, you could move yourself out of your pity party and be useful.*

Although Marsha recognized she was still being unkind to herself with those words, she also recognized the truth of them. Perhaps being who she was couldn't be changed, but she could use it to turn herself into someone that was worth something.

Turning to look at the maple tree outside the window, whose buds were now flying around in the wind making a red haze in the air and a red carpet on the ground, she gathered her courage and texted April asking her permission to go forward with their art center.

Marsha knew that although she felt abandoned, that didn't give her the excuse to abandon the people she could help, even if they didn't know it yet.

And while she was waiting for April's answer, Marsha decided that the next step was to ask for help, and she knew the perfect people to ask.

Ten

Before she could change her mind, Marsha grabbed her purse and walked out the door to Cindy's art gallery. She told herself she could stop at the coffee shop and grab a latte on the way, maybe get everyone coffees and bring them to the gallery.

But the thought of doing that overwhelmed her. First, she had no idea what each of them drank. And the guilt attached to not knowing threatened to take her down into a dark spiral. So she abandoned the idea of coffee for anyone.

The gallery was only a few blocks away from the Ruby House. Which is exactly what April had asked Ron to buy her. She wanted their home to be close enough to walk into the center of town and work at the gallery. So he had done what she had asked, except it was a much bigger house than she had wanted. But then, because of the size, the art center idea had been born.

Marsha pulled her sweatshirt hood over her head and clutched it closed against the wind. The zipper had broken long ago and she hadn't gotten around to fixing it, or getting a new sweatshirt. Or any new clothes. Partly because she kept thinking she didn't want to buy clothes for the weight she was now. All excuses, Marsha knew.

Yes, she definitely needed help. All kinds of help. But first, a discussion with people who understand the art community. Yes, a different medium than dance and theatre. Nevertheless, they knew more than she did.

Although Marsha walked with her head down—partly to keep the wind out of her face, partly to keep people from seeing her, and partly to keep from seeing people—she was still aware of what was around her.

She smelled the coffee shop, and almost went in to get herself a coffee, and then reminded herself how rude that would be to arrive with coffee only for herself. *I'll learn what they drink and bring it next time*, she said to herself.

Marsha walked through the warm, fresh bread scent from the bakery, where Cindy bought bread and bagels. She almost stopped there too, but thinking of her weight, she resisted the urge to go inside.

A flower store had an enormous pot of spring blooms in front. Sprigs of forsythia shining in the sun were shafts of yellow reaching up into the sky. Marsha wondered if there was anyone who didn't smile when seeing flowers.

As Marsha walked, the wind calmed and by the time she reached the gallery, the wind was gone as the weather front moved further east. Glancing up at the now clear blue sky, Marsha whispered a little prayer to whomever might be there, to give her some courage, and then opened the glass door to the gallery. A little bell over the door tinkled, announcing her arrival as she stepped into a spring wonderland.

All the pictures on the wall heralded spring. Flowers of all kinds, in beautiful ceramic and glass vases, stood on pedestals in the corners. The light from the massive windows balanced perfectly with the lights that illuminated the pictures on the walls. Marsha knew that at night, lighting in the ceiling took the place of the natural light, and that too turned the gallery into a magical space.

Marsha realized she was looking at April's touch—a look designed before Ron's secret took her away—and once again felt the massive sorrow sitting on her heart. Heavy and unyielding.

Janet, almost hidden by one of the massive flower arrangements, shouted out, "Marsha, so good to see you," as she practically skipped across the floor. Janet looked like a flower herself. Her spiked hair was tipped pink and green. She wore a purple tunic that floated in the air as she moved, and a light floral scent hung around her. Skinny jeans and pink high-top sneakers completed her outfit.

Without thinking, Marsha breathed out, "Can you make me look that good?"

"Of course she can," her wife Mimi said, coming from the back office. While Janet flowed, Mimi was a rock. Solid. Comforting. And yet so elegant in an easy, natural way, that it almost took Marsha's breath away. Janet's long dark hair hung loose down her back. She wore dark dress pants and a red blouse. No high-top sneakers for her. Instead, a dark shoe with laces and a stacked heel.

Looking at the two of them, living the life they wanted to, partners in all things, Marsha burst into tears, surprising herself. So embarrassed, she turned to leave and then felt Mimi's arm around her, guiding her into what they called the writers' room.

It was a room Cindy had put aside for Janet and Mary to hold their writers' group. But it had grown into more than that. Now it was also used as a comfortable place for anyone to come to curl up on the sofa and read, or just take a brief nap. Cindy knew how important it was to give her employees a place to get away and rest. And Mimi and Janet had turned it into something special.

It was dark, cozy, and comforting. The opposite feeling from the gallery, and yet they belonged together. Through the haze of her feelings, Marsha recognized how the gallery and writers' room represented the two women sitting beside her, holding her hands, waiting for her to gather herself. Not feeling pity or judgment. Just calmly waiting.

That realization made her weep more, this time with yearning and gratitude. Finally, the deep sobs passed, and she blew her nose and wiped her face with the tissues Mimi had handed her.

It was then that Marsha knew that these two women were the people she could tell her secret to. And then she would listen to what they advised. After that, she would ask for more help. With her eating, with the way she looked, with the center.

"Don't you need to watch the door?" Marsha asked.

Mimi gestured to a tablet sitting beside her. She could see the door, and the entire gallery on it.

"If someone comes in, we'll see them. In the meantime, Marsha, can we help you? We are both excellent listeners."

Janet giggled. "And yes, Mimi will do her best to not try to fix anything until you ask her to."

Marsha smiled at the two young women beside her—young enough to have been her daughters, but wise in all the ways she wasn't.

Taking a deep breath, she said, "I want to tell you something I have told no one. Can I start there?"

Both women nodded. Mimi stood and brought two chairs from the desk and put them directly in front of Marsha on the couch. Close enough that their knees were almost touching. Close enough that Marsha could whisper the secret that had been eating away at her for so many years.

Eleven

A month later, Marsha was once again lying on the floor staring at the ceiling after taking herself through an hour of yoga. She smiled. How things had changed. She wasn't just thinking about doing yoga. Or dance. She was doing it.

Telling her secret to Janet and Mimi had opened the door and let her out of the prison where she had put herself. They had cried with her as she told them of the night that Ron Page had raped her. Before Bree. It had been the same as Bree's experience. And even though he had tried to hide who he was, she knew it was Ron.

She was a dancer, an observer of movement. It's how she recognized people before seeing their faces. So she had immediately known it was him from the way he moved.

"Why didn't you say anything?" Janet had asked, squeezing Marsha's hand so hard it hurt. "Why? Your friends would have helped you."

Through her gasping sobs, Marsha had told them why she couldn't. When Ron realized she knew him, he said that if she told anyone, he'd hurt her friends and when he said, "I'll really hurt April," she knew she could never tell.

So for all these years she had lived with the pain of the rape, but also with the terror that Ron would think she told, and then he would hurt April. Even when everyone found out who he was, she still couldn't tell. The secret had crawled into her body and latched itself there.

But with each passing month, now that April was free, she had known that it had to be told. It was eating her alive.

Once the sobs stopped again, Mimi handed Marsha a cup of tea, saying, "Chamomile, it will help." And it had. They had sat together for a few minutes more, as Marsha let the poison from her secret seep out of her body and dissolve into the air.

She could still feel a lump in her heart, though, and she knew what it meant. "I still have to tell April, don't I?"

The women nodded yes.

"But I can't do it over the phone. I have to see her and tell her in person. And although telling you first has made it easier, it still will be one of the hardest things I have ever done."

"You know, of course, it wasn't your fault," Mimi had said. "And she will understand that."

Marsha nodded. "Except I've kept this from her. Maybe for good reasons, but still I did. And when I tell her, won't it open up all the wounds again?"

"It might. But in her heart, April knows that it all has to come out. All that Ron did and who he was must be revealed. She has to know so she can move on. So she can heal from thinking that she should have known."

"And that she loved him," Janet said.

All three women paused for a moment, thinking of what that would feel like. They all loved someone that they knew was good and kind. What would it feel like if they discovered that who they believed them to be wasn't true?

As they sat in silence, Marsha's phone beeped in her purse. Pulling it out, she saw April had answered her text. Holding her breath, she looked at the message and then started crying again. She handed the phone to Janet to see what April had written.

"Marsha, my friend. The Ruby House is as much yours as mine. Go forward with your plans and ideas. When I get home, we can tackle the upstairs together."

A second text came a moment later.

"And for heaven's sake, move into the house. It needs people. Starting with you. I'll join you when I can."

All three women started crying then. April's kindness was so present, even in the middle of her own pain.

It was Janet, who jumped up, her purple tunic lifting and floating like a butterfly as she did so, and said, "Well, let's get started with your makeover, shall we?"

They all laughed then.

"Yes. I'm ready," Marsha had said, realizing that she was. She was ready to move forward in her life. And see where it took her.

And a month later, when she looked in the mirror, she saw a woman on the way to becoming herself. She had lost weight, but had more to lose. Mimi was her accountability partner. The person she called when she wanted to stuff a box of chocolate into her mouth.

Janet and Mimi had sent her to the same person who April had first gone to when she arrived in Spring Falls last year. And then Janet took her shopping. It had taken almost a year to be ready for the change she had come to Spring Falls to find.

But now her straggly brownish gray hair had been lightened and trimmed. She had it piled on the top of her head and felt like the dancer that she had always been. Not yet as thin as she used to be, but as lighthearted as she had been only a few times in her life.

Cindy had hugged Marsha so hard it hurt when Marsha told her she was moving into the Ruby House and finally giving Cindy back her guest room. "You can come back and stay here anytime," Cindy said, trying not to let on that it devastated her she would be alone in the house. Again. As always.

But she said none of that to Marsha. Instead, she asked how she could help, in true Ruby Sister style.

Now the downstairs of the Ruby House was ready for her first dance students, Mimi and Janet. They were her test case, to see if she was ready to teach again, and if they had set the studio up right. They had begged her to at least give them a few basic ballet lessons.

Marsha wasn't sure that they were doing it for themselves, or to force her to get going. Either way, she was both worried and excited to try it. Standing at the window, Marsha could see Mimi and Janet walking up the street heading to the house, holding hands—Janet light on her feet, Mimi solid and strong, making sure Janet didn't float away.

Taking a deep breath, Marsha took one last look in the mirror, folded up her yoga mat and put it in the closet where many yoga mats now lived, and went to the front door to greet her newest students.

What Marsha didn't know was that she was being watched. That throughout her life, she had been watched. And that soon she would meet that person, and it would change her life once again.

Twelve

Sitting in a small cafe in a town she had never heard of before, waiting for her order to arrive at her table, April was wondering if she was ready to return to Spring Falls.

She had already missed the perfect opportunity. The Ruby Sisters had begged her to come home to celebrate her birthday with them. But she couldn't face it.

But now a few more weeks had gone by, and she wondered if she was ready. The traveling had been both painful and inspiring. She had traveled alone for a few weeks, stopping when she wanted to, staying in hotels for days, sobbing into the pillows or watching hours of mindless TV. She'd even tried camping out and decided she hated it.

Actually, that was what the trip had taught her. What she hated. What she liked. She had purchased an iPad along the way and was now journaling every day about what she saw and what she learned about herself. Even the parts she didn't like. April thought that when she looked back on this time in her life, she might call it the big purge.

She was getting better each day. Yes, there were dark days when she had to pull to the side of the road and wait out the rage that coursed through her. Screaming where no one could hear her. Then she'd drive on. Never really having a specific destination. Just going. Just as she had always wanted to live. But Ron had liked order and structure, and she did what made him happy. These days, she was remembering what made her happy.

As she traveled, it felt as if time had disappeared. And she discovered she enjoyed spending moments of time with complete strangers. People she met at gas stations, or restaurants, and even when she was trying out camping. Each new meeting buoyed her spirits. Almost everyone she met was kind, and it reminded her that the world was filled with good people.

"This is my time," she'd yell out the window as she flew down one highway after another. Taking side roads, seeing farms, forests, and cities fly by as if they existed only for her to see them. Sometimes, she'd get the urge to stop and explore, her curiosity leading her.

April realized she had always been afraid to feel pain. So she had avoided painful situations. Bent herself in all kinds of shapes to avoid it. And when the secret that Ron had kept slammed into her like a tidal wave of pain, she thought she couldn't survive it.

But as she drove, she imagined driving away from that tidal wave and letting it draw back and recede. Yes, leaving behind destruction, but not everything had been destroyed. She still had a life waiting for her. The business of designing was still calling her. The thought that the Ruby Sisters had planned her birthday for whenever she returned, because they would not be budged off their love for her, meant she had a safe space to return to.

Yes, it was probably time to go home and face the pain of seeing people who knew the story and would either hate her, pity her, or perhaps try to help. But after weeks of traveling, and purging, and finding herself, she knew she was almost ready.

Just a few weeks more, April said to herself.

"Here you go, ma'am," Ginny Lynn said, putting two coffees and a bagel down in front of April, laughing because they both hated being called ma'am.

April laughed too as her new friend sat down and took half the bagel for herself. April had met Ginny in another small town in another cafe a few weeks before, on her birthday. She had placed a cupcake in front of her, and she was pretending it was a birthday cake.

She had stared at it for so long without touching it that the woman at the next table over had asked, "Is that cupcake sending you a message or what?"

"Kinda," April had answered. "I was wondering if I should go home now or not."

"Home?" the woman asked, and brought her coffee with her over to April's table.

At first April had been offended. Who was this woman invading her space? Then a shiver of fear went through her. But then she realized that was a crazy reaction, part of her pain of the past causing a tiny moment of panic.

Still, she hadn't liked how this woman with huge brown eyes and a red streak in her brown hair had decided she wanted to talk and just barged into her world.

But then April reminded herself she was trying to find herself, and she had loved talking to other strangers. Why not this one? She'd never see this woman again, so she might as well let her into her life for a moment. So April had shared that this was her birthday, and the conversation had flowed from there.

Mostly one sided. The woman introduced herself as Ginny Lynn and then asked all the right questions from April, so she soon found herself prattling away about her trip. She didn't share her past. Just what she was doing in that town, in that cafe, by herself on her birthday.

"Traveling just for the heck of it sounds amazing," Ginny had said. "I always wanted to do that. You've inspired me. Perhaps now is the time.

"Yes," she had said as she tapped her long slender fingers on the table, and picked crumbs off the now empty plate. "Perhaps I'll do it. Be like you, Miss April."

And that had started a traveling friendship. Ginny had said she had some things to do before she could start traveling, but if April could let her know where she was in a few days, she'd meet her there.

And she did. And for the next few weeks, they kept in touch. Each traveling in their own car, going where they wanted to, but if April found herself in a town, she knew she'd stay for a few days, she would text Ginny where she was, and within twenty-four hours, Ginny would show up.

"How are you doing that?" April asked. "How are you going close to where I go when I don't have any idea myself?"

Ginny had reached across the table and held April's hand as she laughed and said, "Psychic, I guess. We must have one of those special connections."

And now that April was thinking of returning home, she had to tell Ginny that her traveling days were over. At least for now. And she had to decide if she would invite Ginny to come with her. And what would the Ruby Sisters think if she brought a friend home?

Ginny smiled at her and asked, "What are you thinking?"

"About going home."

"Oh, awesome. I'll come with you."

And that was that. It was settled. April was going back to Spring Falls and Ginny would follow her there.

Thirteen

He watched as Marsha opened the door and let the two women inside. He stayed as long as he could, hoping to catch glimpses of her as she moved past the window, looking—to him—like a goddess.

It pleased Harry to see that she appeared to be recovering from whatever had been bothering her. Seeing her gain weight and not care about how she looked for the past year had been distressing to him. But what could he do? He was a ghost in her life. Someone that didn't exist.

But that had to change soon. He just couldn't figure out the best way to do it. Which was unusual for him. He made his way in the world telling people what to do and how to do it. How businesses ran and what people needed to do to make them successful was second nature to him.

But the people themselves. That was much harder. Probably because he hadn't cared enough to learn. He didn't need to be liked to be successful. He didn't need to like anyone else either. Or so people believed—as he wanted them to.

The secret he kept to himself was that there were people he liked. Very much. And a few of them knew that, but wisely kept it to themselves. He didn't want to be reminded of his weaknesses, just his strengths. Which were many, and yet so useless when it came to this simple task. Tell her who he was.

"Are you ready, sir?" Amir, his driver, asked. More than a driver. One of the few people he trusted. Amir had been with Harry for years. Harry had demanded perfect loyalty and discretion, and had received it.

"When I am gone, you will be well taken care of," Harry said to the driver. But not out loud. There was no point in being a softy right now. Besides, he was sure that Amir knew. Otherwise, why put up with a man like him?

When he first hired Amir, it never occurred to Harry that perhaps Amir would learn to like him. Why would he?

They were going back to Bruce's office. Bruce had more papers for him to sign. It was taking much longer to get all his affairs in order than he thought it would. And that he was still alive to accomplish it seemed almost like a miracle. It surprised and delighted Harry that he was still here. Perhaps there was a god, after all.

There was another thing that surprised Harry. How much he liked the man Bruce. When Harry was a child, he had a friend or two, but since then, he had not. Too busy, or too involved with what he wanted to do, or too oblivious to the needs of others. *All those reasons,* Harry supposed. But Bruce had become a friend, along with his lawyer, since they had started working together months ago.

Maybe it was because now that Harry struggled just to get up each morning, and move through the day, the small pleasures in life had begun to be important. Like the sun shining through the leaves, and the yellow heads of the daffodils bobbing in the sunlight. Friends.

But most of all, now he felt the pang of loneliness and regret. He could have gotten to know the one person in his life that he had always loved, even though he only knew her from far away and from the reports he had delivered to him weekly about what she was doing. But he didn't really know her. And, of course, Marsha didn't know him at all. He had made sure of that.

But that had to change, and he was still stalling. Never in his life had Harry been as terrified of what he had to do, and he knew he had to do it soon. He had to tell Marsha who he was. Tell her he loved her, and despite appearances, he had always loved her.

But would she ever be able to return that love to him, after all that he had done? Or not done? It was doubtful. But it still had to be done. Soon.

Very soon, he told himself, and Bruce was constantly reminding him.

"You can't put it off any longer, Harry. Not if you want to get to know her. Do it while you still can."

"Sir," Amir said again. This time stepping out of the car and guiding Harry into the back seat. Folding his walker and putting it into the trunk.

Behind the car, where Harry couldn't see him, Amir paused and brushed a tear away. He could never let this crusty, often brusk and impatient man, know how much he cared about him. Watching him waste away was the hardest thing he had ever done.

Not that working for Harry the Hawk had been easy. It never had been. But despite his apparent detachment from human emotions, Harry had been generous and caring about Amir's life. When his wife was ill, it was Harry who made sure she had the best care. When Amir's daughter wanted to go to a special school, it was Harry who made sure that happened.

Yes, Harry was a hard man to work for, but even though he tried hard to not let anyone care about him, almost everyone who had known him through the years loved Harry.

Yes, Amir knew why Harry watched Marsha. He hoped Harry would talk to her soon, and for Harry's sake, that she would see behind the facade and find Harry's true nature, a soft heart that had always loved her. Because that heart was failing.

Fourteen

Marsha squealed with delight at the memory and then started laughing because she felt so happy. She was telling Judith and Bree about her first class teaching again. And what Janet and Mimi were like as they learned basic ballet moves. And most of all, how much she loved the entire experience.

Everything. The room, the house, the women, the teaching. Everything.

"So you liked everything about it?" Judith asked.

"I just said I did, didn't I?" Marsha snapped, and then laughed again.

"Oh, sarcasm. Imagine that! But, yes. I liked everything about it."

The three of them were having lunch together to catch up. Cindy couldn't join them this time. She had a meeting with a new artist and couldn't put it off.

So it was just the three of them at ParaTi's. Mary had delivered their food, and then said her shift was over and then leaned over to kiss her mother's cheek.

Watching them, Judith felt the rise of emotions and the threat of tears—emotions that were happening more and more often. Judith put it down to the fact that she was in a genuine relationship for the first time in her life, and that had opened a door to more feelings. She wasn't sure that was a good or bad thing, but there was nothing she was going to do to stop it. She was keeping Bruce in her life.

Marsha's excitement about teaching again added to Judith's happiness. For so long, she had been worried about Marsha, wondering what was going on and if she would ever get over it. But now that Marsha had moved into the Ruby House, and was teaching again, Judith figured she had nothing to worry about with Marsha. She was on her way to building a new life.

After Mary left, waving at all of them, Bree looked at all of them and smiled, and Judith realized she had never seen Bree this happy before either. The traveling must have been good for her.

Bree had returned from her impulsive trip last week. The trip had lasted much longer than Bree had thought it would. She thought she would only be gone a week, but after visiting Longwood Gardens, she just kept driving. She had written emails and was face-timing while she was gone, so no one would worry. Besides, they could see her progress as she zig-zagged her way around the country, following some inner directive.

Bree had thought about April, wondering if they would run across each other as they drove around. But every time she looked at her app, she saw they were moving in opposite directions. Bree stayed away from crowds and noise, and observed the people she saw. Sometimes she exchanged smiles and nods, but if she had to talk, she kept the conversations short. Mostly she kept to herself and watched, gathering ideas, listening in on conversations, and studying how people related to each other.

Bree continued to visit gardens. She would talk to the spring flowers and blooming trees, working out things she had not had the time, or the emotional energy, to deal with before.

Sometimes Bree stopped for a few days and wrote. Bree told the Ruby Sisters that it felt like she was on a moving writer's retreat. It was just what she needed. And now she was back and still writing. The book's first draft was almost done, and she was waiting for a week or two to revise it.

Which meant she was spending time in her garden, and with Mary and her family. And catching up with friends. Seeing Marsha so happy after watching her swing through moods the past year was a relief. It meant they were all back on track.

Including April. She had texted them all a few days before and said she'd be home by the weekend. And she was expecting a birthday party. And then a few minutes later she had added that she was bringing a friend named Ginny Lynn.

And yes, they would have to reserve their curiosity until they got there. "So don't bug me with questions," she had added just in time. Because every single Ruby Sister was ready to text her and ask who this Ginny was and where they met.

Instead, they sent heart emojis and talked together, trying to discern what April was up to. But since they didn't know, they tried to only focus on the fact that April was coming home, and it was time to plan a party. Which was another reason they were having lunch together.

"Of course, the party has to be at the Ruby House. It's ready. All we need is food and decorations," Marsha said.

"And we need to know when she is actually coming home," Judith added. "I'll drag it out of her. I'll tell her that if she doesn't give us a time, there won't be a party."

Marsha laughed, knowing how April hated to be pinned down to timing. She was so happy about April coming home she thought she would burst. The only sour note was April bringing a friend. Someone who would stay in the other bedroom at The Ruby House.

April had texted asking Marsha to make sure it was ready for a guest. It didn't have to be perfect. They could all start working on the upstairs design together.

Something about the whole friend thing bugged Marsha, but she didn't know why. So she shrugged off her feelings about it and asked Judith how Bruce was doing with his new house, and moving his estate planning business to Spring Falls.

"Great. And the community college is talking to him about teaching a course. Which he is ecstatic about. Said he didn't know he wanted to teach until they asked him. And he has a few new clients. Nancy says he is fairly busy, especially with some old guy named Harry Harrison."

"Who's he?"

Judith shrugged? "Don't know. I asked him, and he said he couldn't tell me much, because he's a client. Which, of course, I understand. But still. All I can tell is the guy has a lot of estate planning to do, and Bruce likes him."

"Have you met him?" Bree asked.

"Not yet. But they have scheduled a meeting with me. Turns out Mr. Harrison might also have need of my services."

"And then you won't be able to tell us anything either," Marsha said.

"True," Judith responded, and then had the thought that might be why they were meeting. To keep her from investigating and then telling her friends who this Harry guy was.

Probably not, she thought. *But I'll wait and see.*

Fifteen

Judith stared at the two men sitting across from her. In all of her life, she had rarely been astonished. Surprised maybe when she uncovered something a client had done. Usually unintentionally. Angry when she uncovered deception of any kind.

But astonished? This was something that rocked her back in her chair and made her suck in her breath. She wanted to slap herself to find out if she was dreaming, but she knew she wasn't. She was in her office and it was the middle of the day.

She had closed the blinds entirely, not needing to put Bruce or his client in the spotlight. She had been curious about what was to come, and as always happy to see Bruce.

Nancy had opened the door for the two of them. The man was leaning heavily on Bruce's arm. It had touched Judith to see how carefully Bruce helped the old man into his chair, making sure he was comfortable before sitting down himself. Judith knew Bruce was picky about friends, and although the man was clearly his client, it was obvious that he cared about him.

The man had nodded his head at her and said, "Excuse me for not rising to shake your hand, but I am delighted to meet you.

Bruce has told me a little about you, and I was looking forward to getting to know you.

"I'm sure you know my name is Harry Harrison, and that I have been working with Bruce to put my affairs in order.

"It's been much more complicated than I thought it would be. I am part owner and the primary owner of a variety of businesses, most of them wildly successful. This happened because when I started out in business, I decided that if I was going to be an adviser to a business, that I should get paid for their future growth. Although I often was wrong, I was more often right."

Harry paused, coughed, and Bruce handed him a glass of water that Nancy had set on the desk for them. Smiling at Bruce and patting his hand, Harry continued.

"I suppose it's obvious that I am not only old, I am also sick. The prediction was I should have died a month ago, but knowing that I have unfinished business has probably kept me alive. And Bruce. Best friend I ever made."

Bruce turned away then, and Judith, knowing Bruce, knew he was trying to hide the swell of emotions that statement caused in him. When he turned back to Harry, he said, "Thank you. That means more than I can say."

After another coughing spell, Harry continued.

"Bruce has almost finished with my estate. We have moved most of my assets to charities that I have worked with over the years. I have taken care of the staff that has served me. But there is one person I want to take care of, but I don't know how to go about it. And that's where Bruce suggested you could help me."

"Why me?"

"Because you are her friend. I don't just want to leave her money. I want to get to know her, before I leave this life. But I am afraid. Something that is foreign to me, I admit. Fear has never gotten in my way before. What's that saying, 'Feel the fear and do it any way?'

That's what I've always done, in business anyway. I always seemed to know the right thing to do in business. But in life, I am afraid I have failed.

"And now, this late in life, I want something I might not be able to have, and this is where I hope you will help me."

"I can try. But who are you talking about, and how do you want me to help?"

"Marsha. I want to meet Marsha."

"Marsha? Why?"

"She's my daughter."

"Marsha's your daughter?"

Judith had stared at Bruce and Harry, trying to figure out what to say. Would this destroy Marsha or help her? Should she say yes to help, or tell this man to take his sad story somewhere else?

Neither man said anything. After her long moment of astonishment, and wondering if she had just dreamed what she heard, Judith stood and walked out of the room, saying, "Excuse me, I'll be back in a moment."

Walking past Nancy, who started to ask what was happening, Judith stepped out into the street and took a deep breath. It was midafternoon. A breeze that carried a hint of rain ruffled her hair. Dark clouds were hastening across the blue sky.

Nancy stood at her desk watching her boss stand as still as a statue, hands clenched at her side, head bowed. She couldn't decide if she should go outside and see if Judith needed her, or into the office to see if the two men were okay.

Just as she was about to do the former, Judith returned, face as pale as Nancy had ever seen it, but her red hair flaming the way it did when she was determined and opened the office door.

Good lord, Nancy thought. *Someone is in trouble.*

• • • ● ● • ● ● • •

The rain Judith had smelled arrived a few minutes later at the same time Cindy's phone rang.

"Could you come to my office?" Judith asked.

"Now?"

"Now."

Cindy grabbed her purse and calling back to Mimi and Janet that she had to run out, took an umbrella out of the stand by the front door and literately ran to Judith's office.

The last time Judith had called her to the office this way it was to meet Nicky Blair, the women who led them all to the truth about Ron. What could possibly be happening now?

Please, don't let it be something terrible like that, Cindy said to herself as she hopped a puddle that had already formed, happy she had worn sneakers that day instead of heels.

Nancy was waiting for her at the door, took her umbrella and pointed to the office. "In there."

"What's going on?"

"Don't know, but it is either really good or really bad."

"Great," Cindy muttered under her breath.

But when she heard the story, she had the same reaction as Judith. Astonished, and not able to decide if it was good or bad. But it was definitely really something.

Sixteen

Once April was only a few hours from Spring Falls, she began to panic. If Ginny hadn't been following her, she might have turned her car around and gone anywhere else. Maybe to California. She'd never been there. She heard the sun was always shining there, except lately. *Nothing is the same anymore, is it?* April said to herself.

Certainly not in her life. That was the problem. Wherever she went, she would be there. So she could keep traveling forever, but would that change anything?

The voice in her head kept telling her she wasn't ready to go home. And she kept telling it to be quiet. Her heart was leading her there, and that was how it was going to be, no matter how afraid she was. Because going back to where everyone knew her scared the bejesus out of her.

When she first left her daughter's house, the pain would sometimes make her pull over and weep for hours. But then she got into the rhythm of traveling and that pain came with her but didn't stir up her emotions in the same way.

April loved the anonymity of traveling. It had been wonderful meeting people who did not know who she was. She called herself May Zane, using her maiden name. She never said where she was from. If they insisted, she said her daughter and her family lived in Canada, implying that she lived there too.

But back in Spring Falls, even changing her name couldn't change anything. She would still be Ron Page's wife. Ron Page, mass murderer still at large, now on the top ten most wanted list. He was infamous, and that made her the subject of hate and ridicule, and sometimes pity, which in some ways was worse.

Judith had promised her it wouldn't be that way. She would be who she always was to them. Their friend.

"Who you were married to didn't turn you into someone else," Judith had assured her.

"But I didn't know," April had wailed on the phone to Judith. "I should have known."

Judith, calm and as determined as always, had answered, "None of us knew, April. None of us. Even those of us who knew more about Ron didn't know how bad it was."

April knew Judith was referring to Bree. If Bree would have told them all what Ron had done to her, would she have married him? When April had first asked herself that question, she had been positive that she wouldn't have. Which made her furious with Bree for keeping that from her.

But as the months slid by, April wondered if that was true. Perhaps she would have done what Bree had worried about. She would have never spoken to any of the Ruby Sisters again. She would have sided with Ron.

But I'll never know, will I, April mumbled to herself. *No one trusted me enough to tell me the truth. And even though I still had the Ruby Sisters, I moved away from them, and none of us spoke to Bree again for all those years.*

Or really to Marsha, either, she thought to herself. Marsha moved away too, and barely communicated with them for years. Until they all got the letter from Paul, asking them to help Bree.

What if he did that to Marsha too, and she never said? The thought came so clearly to April that she knew it must be true. She was so startled, she swerved, almost hitting a car that was passing her.

No, she said to herself. *I don't believe it. It was another reason.*

And although she shut that thought down, it lingered in the back of her mind, and April knew it was just one more thing she would have to confront when she returned.

I am returning to the scene of the crime, April muttered to herself. Although she had to pee, she kept driving, afraid that if she stopped for a moment, she wouldn't keep going.

Which meant as soon as she reached Judith's, where she and Ginny would be staying, she would have to dash into the house instead of getting one of Judith's famous all embracing hugs.

She could have gone to the Ruby House. Marsha had told her that their rooms were ready, but she then changed her mind and started again at Judith's. Just as she had done the year before.

As she drove, April thought about Judith's house with the warm cinnamon buns in the morning and the feeling of confidence and security Judith always brought to everything. April knew she could sleep in as long as she wanted, huddled away from facing anything for a little longer.

Judith could meet Ginny and keep her company, introduce her around for her. Ginny said she'd stay for a few days just to meet her friends and then move on.

"Move on to where?" April had asked.

"Not sure yet," Ginny had answered. Which made April realize she didn't know much about Ginny. Which was another reason for going to Judith's first. Judith would unearth what they needed to know about Ginny.

And now that she had that thought about Marsha and Ron, April was doubly glad she wasn't staying at the Ruby House. It meant she could put off asking that question of Marsha and hearing the answer.

Judith had asked April when she wanted her belated birthday party and she had said she'd decide when she got there. Yes, she wanted to see everyone. Yes, she wanted a party. But the idea of all that happiness combined with worrying about her seemed too much to deal with at the moment.

One step at a time, April said to herself. *One mile at a time. I can do it.*

Behind her, Ginny flashed her lights. It was her signal that she needed a pit stop.

Sighing, April flipped her turn signal into the gas station, thinking it was probably better this way. She really needed to pee. And Ginny would keep her from turning around. Because it was Ginny who insisted that April was ready.

"Besides," Ginny had said, "Your friends sound amazing. I can't wait to meet them."

April had answered automatically, "I can't wait to introduce you to them," and then wondered to herself if that was true.

Seventeen

Ginny Lynn bit her fingernails on one hand while driving with the other. It was a terrible habit. One that she had tried throughout her entire life to quit. At least when she got old enough to recognize that it was a bad habit. And it made her weak in front of others.

The mean girls in school would look at her ragged nails and laugh at her, calling her trailer trash. It wasn't just her nails. She was a target, no matter what she did.

And it was all her best friend's fault. Even now, years later, Ginny felt the urge to scream at the betrayal. One day they were friends, the next they weren't. Why? Because her best friend discovered that the mean girls had power.

When Ginny was feeling gracious, which wasn't often, she realized that the choice was fairly obvious. Who could blame her friend? She could either have stuck with the skinny, short girl with dull brown hair, and no genuine talent for anything, or go with the girls who knew everyone, looked beautiful, and ruled the high school.

It was really a matter of survival. So her friend left Ginny to fend on her own against them. *Which made me who I am today*, Ginny thought. *She would show them. Who was trailer trash now?*

She had tracked down many of those girls and knew what they had become. Her best friend had gotten fat and lazy with a few bratty kids and a cheating husband to deal with. The mean girls ended up in real life where their kind of power didn't last long against people who were better at bullying and manipulating than they were. A few of them made something of themselves. Most didn't.

Unlike me, Ginny thought. *I am somebody now. My own person. I decide what my life will be like every day.*

Which was one reason she enjoyed befriending April and traveling with her, and now would go with her to Spring Falls. April was a woman who had no mean bone in her body, but was the target of the grown up mean girls and boys who loved putting down others, because—although they didn't know it—they were completely useless themselves. They lived off the world, but made no difference to it.

Yes, the minute she met April, she added another reason to befriend her. She would protect her against the world. Well, at least from the mean men and women of the world. Which was why she was now following her to some town in the middle of nowhere. That and the other reason. But the other reason was her secret to keep. At least for a while.

A few months ago, Spring Falls had been the center of a news story that she, like everyone else, had followed. Then she had an opportunity to do more than follow the story, and she took it.

When Ginny first met May Zane, she pretended she didn't know who she really was, April May Zane Page. Ginny had to wait until they got to know each other before April told her the story, and Ginny had to pretend that she hadn't known.

Ginny was careful about how she dealt with April. She never treated her as anything other than someone she met on the road. Someone she wanted to be friends with. And when April decided to return to Spring Falls, Ginny made sure April invited her to come along with her and visit.

Going to Spring Falls with April was an opportunity that would change her life. It was why Ginny had been following behind April's car for hours, and getting increasingly anxious about what April's friends would think about her.

Hence, the nail biting. Which she had under control until she met April.

Everything will be okay. They will all do what you want them to do. Ginny said to herself. Over and over again, keeping her mind busy and her hands firmly on the steering wheel and not moving towards her mouth. She had also popped a stick of gum in her mouth to stop the biting. Ginny actually hated chewing gum, but it kept her teeth busy.

For the past half hour, she had needed a bathroom break and had assumed April would need to stop too. But when April showed no signs of pulling over, she gave up and flashed her lights. As Ginny parked, she watched April get out of her car and head into the gas station without even a wave. A sure sign that she had been trying to force herself to keep driving, even though she needed to use the restroom, too.

Following her into the station, she saw April's fluffy brown hair bobbing in front of her. Ginny knew that when people saw them together, they thought they might be mother-daughter, or perhaps sisters.

Both of them had big brown eyes, almost the same color hair, although April's had some gray in it. Ginny was a few inches taller than April, although that didn't take much. April had told Ginny the Ruby Sisters sometimes called her little wren, and Ginny could see why, especially when April's burden of sorrow and guilt lifted for a moment.

Ginny thought one reason April had so quickly accepted her as a friend was because they looked enough alike for Ginny to feel familiar to her. When April told her about returning to Spring Falls, Ginny had invited herself, saying she'd stay for a few days and then head back out on the road.

But that hadn't been quite true. She had only said that so April wouldn't worry about bringing her along. However, Ginny planned to stay in Spring Falls as long as she needed to.

Instead of being an outcast, she'd be part of something. Something that would make her famous.

One can always dream, can't they? Ginny asked herself.

When April came out of the bathroom, they high-fived each other. Before Ginny closed the bathroom door, she watched April head to the counter to buy some snacks. Ginny knew April well enough that she knew April would buy her a snack and drink, too. That was April. Gracious even when she was worried.

Who wouldn't want a friend like that? Ginny thought, as she closed the door and locked it.

Eighteen

"What do you want us to do Harry?" Judith asked as soon as she had finished telling Cindy what Harry had told them. Harry had listened while leaning back in his chair, breathing heavily, eyes half closed.

Judith had asked Cindy to come to her office because she counted on Cindy being more calm and gracious than she would be, and that was exactly what had happened. Once Cindy heard Harry was Marsha's father, Cindy stood and gently held one of Harry's hands, leaned over and gave him a kiss on his cheek. Harry's eyes had filled with tears.

"How wonderful is this? Won't Marsha be delighted?" Cindy said, sitting down on the chair Judith had placed beside her desk, her face glowing with happiness for Marsha.

Judith looked at her friend and asked, "Are you sure?"

It was only then that Cindy realized that Marsha might have an entirely different and opposite reaction. They all knew that Marsha's mother had told her she didn't need to know who her father was. And then drank herself to death because he had left her.

"Maybe not?"

Which was when Judith asked, "What do you want us to do, Harry?"

Harry took a ragged breath before answering. "If you were asking me a business question, I would know exactly what I want and I would be positive I could accomplish it. But ask a question involving my daughter who doesn't know me, and I don't think it matters what I want."

"Maybe not, Harry, but if we are going to help you, we need to know what you wish would happen." Cindy said.

"If I could have everything I want—which I accept is unlikely to happen—I would want Marsha to be delighted to know me, and I could spend my last days with her. She'd forgive me for not coming forward before, and she would find some love in her heart for me.

"Will it happen that way? Probably not. But what I can't see is me telling her. If she walked away, what could I do, run after her?

"So what I want is for you to tell her. That way, she'd have time to think things through with all of you. Then when she isn't too angry, perhaps then we could meet.

"I know I can't expect her to forgive me for staying away. All my reasons seem both cold and stupid now."

Judith thought to herself that he was probably right, and if he wasn't an old dying man, she would have told him so. Just because. But Bruce's look reminded her she couldn't make everything perfect all the time.

So instead of saying what she thought, Judith asked, "Where have you been all this time?"

Harry looked at Bruce before answering.

"Tell them."

Harry sighed. "Near here. Except when I moved to New York when she lived there, and again close to the town where Marsha was teaching when she moved there. When she came back here, I returned."

"Why did you do that when you didn't want her to know who you were? Why not just stay away?"

"I was trying to do what her mother asked me to do. Stay out of her life. And I did. But I wanted to at least watch Marsha grow up. I wanted to be near her. I was in the audience at almost all her recitals and plays. I went to her graduation. And if I couldn't be there, I had someone else there for me to take pictures and movies."

Smiling at the thought, Harry added, "I have quite a collection."

"I can't figure out if that is creepy or wonderful. Maybe both," Judith said. "And I still don't get why you did that. Why not just be in her life? I don't understand why Marsha's mother told you to stay out of Marsha's life. Are you a terrible man? Have you committed crimes?"

Once again, Harry looked at Bruce, who nodded.

"Her mother and I used to be best friends. We met in college. She said she loved me, and I loved her, too, but in my own way. We did almost everything together, and one night I gave in to her desire for us to be more than friends and we slept together. And amazingly, she got pregnant. I was so happy. I couldn't believe I would get to have a child.

"She was happy at first, too. But when I told her I didn't love her the way she wanted me to, she demanded that I leave and never see her or the child again."

Harry stopped to cough and then took a minute to get his breath back.

"It broke my heart, but I promised. And I kept that promise in a way. But I couldn't not see my child. It was too much to ask of me."

"Sorry, but I still don't get it, Harry. Why would she make you stay away? What did you do that would make her demand that of you?" Cindy said.

Judith glanced at Cindy and then Bruce before saying, "I think I know. It's because you were—are—gay."

Bruce took over for Harry, who started wheezing in his chair too much to answer.

"Marsha's mother was brought up to believe that being gay was the devil's work. She felt betrayed by a man she thought loved her and she thought she was damned forever by participating in an unholy act.

"Even now, all these years later, you know how people can be. Harry agreed to stay away because he was trying to protect his daughter from the embarrassment of having a gay father. And once it became a little more accepted, too many years had gone by to just walk up and tell her."

Harry sipped the water Cindy had handed him and rasped out an answer. "It's true. I thought I was doing Marsha a favor. But I was fooling myself. It was wrong, and I have to fix it before I die."

Cindy and Judith looked at each other, both of them wondering exactly how Marsha would take this news.

"I understand, Harry, but let me clarify what you want us to do. You want us to tell Marsha for you?"

"Please."

Judith let out a breath and then looked at Cindy, and then Bruce.

"Okay. But not for you, Harry. For Marsha. And because you look like you are going to keel over at any moment. I agree that Marsha should have the opportunity to choose, and yes, if you tell her, she might shut you out and she'd never have the chance to work through this for herself.

"So for Marsha, we'll do it. If it works out for you too, that would be wonderful. But you have to know that Marsha comes first for us."

Harry stood, leaning heavily on Bruce. "Thank you. It's all I can ask."

As Bruce helped Harry out of the office, into the waiting car, he looked back at Cindy and Judith and tilted his head. Cindy smiled back. Judith just stared at him. Exactly as he expected.

But Bruce had come to care for this man, and he hoped that Judith and Cindy could work a miracle and bring Harry and his daughter together before it was too late.

Nineteen

As soon as the door closed behind Bruce and Harry, both Cindy and Judith's phone beeped with a new text message.

"Yay!" Cindy said, looking at the phone. "April is almost here!"

Nancy, knowing what question Judith would ask next, said, "Nope, you have no more clients today."

"Do you want to come with me?" Judith asked Cindy.

Judith couldn't wait to see April, but she was worried. What would April look like? Would she say the right things to her?

She knew Cindy was better at saying the right things in times like this than she was. And Cindy would keep her from demanding straight out who April's friend was.

Judith hated to admit it, but she felt a tightening in her stomach that she always got when she worried about something. She was afraid of what April might be getting herself into. She was worried that April had invited some dangerous stranger into her life and into their home.

Of course, it could be a wonderful thing, she told herself. And that was why she had to keep her mouth shut. She didn't want to spoil what could be what April needed most.

Both Bree and Marsha texted Judith, having also gotten April's text, and asked if they should come to Judith's to welcome April home.

Judith's first thought was no, it was too much. But then why did April tell everyone if she didn't want to see them? Perhaps she wanted to get the awkwardness over as soon as possible.

"Everybody?" Judith asked Cindy.

"I think so. I think it's what she wants."

So, thirty minutes later, as April pulled up to Judith's house, all the Ruby Sisters were waiting for her.

The car had barely come to a stop before April flung open the door and ran towards them. They met in the middle of the lawn, everyone hugging her, crying and laughing at the same time.

Seconds later, a cloud passed over the sun, sending down a shower of rain on the five of them. As they ran towards the open garage door, April turned and waved to the woman in the car that had pulled up behind her to follow them.

In the car, Ginny waved back, but remained in the car for a moment to gather her thoughts. She knew who these women were. After all, she had asked April many times to describe her friends. She had encouraged her to talk about what was special about each of them, making mental notes, so she almost felt as if she knew them now.

Ginny doubted April knew how much she had told her because she was careful. She never asked too many questions at one time and slipped them into casual conversations. At first, April had been reluctant to share, but, as Ginny knew she would, April felt more and more comfortable about sharing small things with her about each of her friends.

Ginny now knew how each of them had met, what they did for work, and what they believed in. She knew what April perceived as each of their strengths and weaknesses. Ginny knew April saw herself as too rigid when she was afraid, and that was what she felt had kept her from seeing who Ron was. April had described each of her friends so accurately that Ginny knew who each of them was as she watched them hug and then run into the garage to get out of the rain.

She saw Marsha, the tall dancer. Judith with the red hair who challenged everything until it was right. *Someone for me to be afraid of for sure,* she thought. She saw Bree, the writer, standing a little separately, smiling and observing, and Cindy, the one who wanted to help everyone, clapping and jumping for joy at the sight of her friend.

For a moment, Ginny felt such an intense jealousy at what she was watching she couldn't move. Her hand on the door handle getting ready to run into the rain, she told herself to stop it. She was here for April. Everything else could be forgotten.

As Ginny rushed up the driveway, April ran out to get her and pulled her into the garage with the rest of them. A moment later, the rain stopped as abruptly as it had started and Bree pointed out a rainbow that hung over the house across the street.

Everything sparkled as the tiny drops of rain reflected the light. The air smelled fresh and carried a hint of lilac from a bush blooming in the neighbor's yard. It was a beautiful moment, everyone smiling at each other. They were together again.

But Judith couldn't shake her worry. She had the oddest thought that the woman April was introducing as Ginny had brought the rain with her. Was it a warning? Or was it a good thing? After all, April showers bring May flowers. And here was April May Zane, finally home again.

It has to be a good thing, Judith said to herself. *I am worrying about nothing.*

April introduced Ginny to each Ruby Sister, getting to Judith last. As she shook hands with Ginny, Judith couldn't help but notice how much April and Ginny looked like each other. Sure, Ginny was a little taller and younger, but they definitely could be mother and daughter.

Maybe that's what attracted April to Ginny, Judith thought. *Attracted?* Judith asked herself. *That's a weird word to use.*

"Let's go inside," Judith said, ushering them through the garage door into the house.

"I'll get the bags," Marsha said, and started down the driveway before anyone could stop her.

As she held open the door for the women, Judith watched Marsha get April's bags from the car. Something was bothering Marsha. Was it because April was home, or because she brought someone with her?

There I am worrying again, Judith noticed. It has to stop. But then, remembering what she had to tell Marsha, she sighed. Perhaps that was what was bothering her. Marsha's life was about to change.

But not right now. This was April's time.

Judith held the door for Marsha as she brought in April's bags and smiled at her. Marsha tried to smile back, but it didn't reach her eyes. *Yes,* Judith thought, something is bothering her. *Was it because April brought someone home?*

Maybe not. Judith said to herself. *Maybe I am just imagining things.*

But Judith didn't really believe that. Something was up, and eventually she'd find out what it was, because she always did.

Twenty

A few days later, they held the promised birthday party at the art gallery instead of the Ruby House. Cindy wanted to welcome April home in style, so with Janet and Mimi's help she had gone all out with the decorations. Seth had come over to hang the silver curly streamers from the beams. After Janet's attempt to hang holiday decorations, he had made them promise to always call him when they needed to hang something from the beams.

Silver helium balloons were anchored in all the corners, a big happy birthday sign was strung across the wall in front of all the paintings, and a table filled with food sat in the middle of the gallery floor. There were even April's favorite peanut butter and banana chip sandwiches.

A *closed* sign hung on the door with the promise that they would be open in a few hours. They had tried to keep Mittens in the office, but she wailed at being locked in, and was now curling herself around everyone's legs purring loudly. Every time April sat down, Mittens would hop into her lap and stare at her.

"Are you trying to tell me something, Mittens?" April had asked, the first time it had happened.

"She's trying to tell you she missed you and not to go away again like that," Janet had said. "Just like us."

Janet, her blond hair currently tipped a brilliant neon pink, could have said more, but they both knew it wasn't necessary. It was an unspoken agreement with all of them to not bring up why April left, but to only celebrate her return.

So even though they called it a birthday celebration, it was really a welcome home.

They had waited a few days to hold the party, giving April time to rest and be home without a lot of fanfare. Having coffee and cinnamon buns in Judith's garden had been the first thing she had asked for, and she and Judith had talked quietly about what had been going on in town while April was gone.

They also talked about April's children, but not Ron. April's son, Robert, had written her an email apologizing for leaving, and the two of them were having more communication than they had for many years. He sent texts with pictures of where he was, and April loved showing them to everyone.

She also shared pictures of her new grandson, which, now that she was out of their hair, her daughter was sending to her almost every day. April told Judith that she felt as if she was getting to know her children now. Neither one of them mentioned it was Ron who had kept her separate from the children because he wanted all the attention.

During their talks in the garden, Judith had been grateful that Ginny had stayed in her room, giving them the privacy they needed. In fact, she had stayed out of all the Ruby Sisters' way the last few days.

Judith wished she didn't have a suspicious heart, that she could just accept that Ginny was just being friendly. But she couldn't. Something bothered her about the situation, and she hoped Ginny would move on soon.

Now, at the party, she watched Ginny work the room. Not in an obvious way, glad-handing everyone. It was much more subtle. Very skilled. Especially for someone so young. Ginny spoke with everyone in a style that made them comfortable. Except two people. Judith and Marsha.

To Judith, Mittens looked as if she was actively avoiding Ginny, too. She half expected to see Mittens hiss at Ginny. Instead, Mittens glared at Ginny anytime she came near, and then would turn and lift her tail as she walked away. It made Judith laugh every time she saw it. It was exactly what she felt like doing—if she had a tail.

Marsha accommodated Ginny, probably for April's sake. But Judith could see how stiffly she held herself even as she smiled and chatted.

"Observing the room as usual?" Bruce said, coming to stand beside her, holding a glass of what looked like champagne but was really flavored sparkling water. It was an unspoken agreement that the Ruby Sisters had since they were in high school, that they wouldn't serve alcohol at Ruby Sister parties. Both Bree and Marsha had too many bad memories surrounding it.

Judith leaned into Bruce ever so slightly and felt immediately comforted.

"Yes, I guess I am."

"You know you can't make everything be perfect all the time."

"I know. But still. It's good to keep watch, don't you think?"

"It doesn't matter if I think it's good or not, does it? That is what you do. And I am here supporting you while you do it."

Judith reached down and held Bruce's hand. She didn't have to say that she loved him for it. He already knew that.

So the two of them watched the room together. They saw Mimi, her long dark hair piled in some elaborate way on the top of her head, laugh with Janet as they watched Mittens bat at a balloon.

Mimi and Janet were also standing together, holding hands. They tipped their glasses filled with lemonade at Bruce and Judith when they saw them watching.

Bruce and Judith saluted back with their glasses.

"The party is perfect, isn't it?" Cindy asked, coming up to them. "April seems at peace. She says she is coming back to work in the gallery starting next week. Which makes me extremely happy.

"And she said she and Marsha and Seth will move forward with the Ruby House makeover. I think Marsha has some ideas of what to do that need April's attention."

The three of them turned to watch the party and laughed at Rho, in her mother's arms, mesmerized by the silver streamers. All three of them saw the dark car go slowly past the gallery and they knew who was inside, and why.

"You know you can't put it off much longer," Bruce said. "She has to know, and have time to process it."

Judith and Cindy nodded, knowing that Bruce was right. It was time.

"Tomorrow?" Judith asked.

"Everyone, or just us?"

"I think just us for now." Judith answered, thinking of Ginny and how she didn't want her involved at all. Besides, Marsha was already upset about something, and too many people might feel like an intervention.

"How about at your house, Cindy? She's comfortable there."

"Okay," Cindy said, sighing, not looking forward to it.

"Let's think of it this way," Judith said, knowing exactly how Cindy felt. "It might be hard to hear at first, but it could be just what Marsha needs right now."

"Okay. I'll think of it that way. And right now, it's time to play a little music, dance a little, eat a lot of food, and celebrate!"

"I'll drink to that," Bruce said, lifting his glass, and headed out into the crowd to hug a few people, dragging Judith with him.

"Time to participate, young lady," he whispered.

"Yes, sir!" Judith mock saluted and headed off to talk to that "Ginny girl" as she called her to find out what she could about the stranger who Judith knew wanted in to their circle, even though she hadn't said so.

The question was, should they let her in or not?

Twenty One

Ginny was thoroughly enjoying herself. She hadn't been in a group of people this lively and happy in a long time. Probably never, actually.

The people she knew were always in a rush to meet deadlines. There were only a few acceptable topics of conversation. Nothing deep or interesting.

Home and family were topics if it made the person look important. Topics like how their kid was just elected as president of his class. No mention of how much money his parents put into making sure that was the outcome.

Or if their house was going to be in Architectural Digest. A house that was so big a small town could live in it, when there were only two adults and one perfect child living there. None of whom were home enough to call it an actual home. Their staff enjoyed it instead.

Ginny thought how different her life had been from the lives of her work acquaintances. Her home had been so small it could fit in one of their kitchens. But her parents always filled the house with interesting ideas and delightful smells. Even though they had little to smile about, they smiled anyway at each other and tried to find the good in it all.

For a moment, Ginny faltered in her resolve, remembering who she used to be. Loved. Valued. A good person.

However, when all of that was taken away from her, she had to adapt. A car accident—one that could have been avoided—and she was an orphan. Not important to anybody anymore. And she became determined to change that no matter what it took.

She was young, smart, and pretty enough, and she had worked her way quickly into a job she enjoyed. She became someone again—maybe not loved, but at least important. Until she screwed it up.

However, she was in the process of repairing that screwup. She'd be part of that inner circle again, no matter what it took, or who she had to become. Which was why she was expertly working the room at this ridiculous party, even if she had to admit that she was enjoying it. And that kinda pissed her off. She wanted to just be working, not liking the people.

But their happiness was contagious, and their conversations were interesting. At the parties and gatherings she used to attend, besides bragging about family, work was the only allowed topic of conversation. Which she wouldn't have minded, but it got old quickly, listening to people who didn't know what they were talking about, but acted as if they did.

What she had learned was that the people who had something worthwhile to discuss were not the ones acting like pompous fools. They were the ones who watched and listened, and only shared when it was the right time and place.

And in this room, even though she hadn't expected it, she realized that it was filled with people who cared about each other and had ideas to talk about. Not gossip. Not slander. Ideas.

She kept trying to disprove that to herself, but was failing, and it scared her a little because she was starting to feel like her old self again, and she couldn't afford that. And what made it even more difficult was that these people were people she was sure her parents would have liked.

They would have invited them into their tiny house, sat around the kitchen table with all its nicks and scratches, and drunk coffee and laughed and talked about things that made a difference.

But, Ginny reminded herself, she was not her parents. She was not here to become part of this group for longer than necessary.

She knew that Judith and her friend, the nice-looking man holding her hand, were suspicious of her. And so was the dang cat. But she'd win them over. She had won over April, hadn't she?

At first it was because they celebrated April's birthday together with that lonely cupcake, and April had shared some of her life, thinking she'd never see Ginny again.

But it was the moment they both laughed at being called ma'am and shared that first bagel she knew April would eventually like her and not think of her as a stranger. How could April not like and accept Ginny? She was designed to be a younger April. It was perfect.

Sometimes Ginny even felt like April's daughter. Which was good up to a point, but it couldn't be carried too far. She'd never get her job done if she let herself feel that way too long.

However, when she turned to look at April smiling and being hugged by her friends, she had trouble keeping her feelings apart from her work. Although April didn't look like her mother, she had that same light-hearted way about her.

And that fact interested Ginny. What if her lighthearted, generous mother had married a man like Ron Page? Would she have recognized what he really was? Would she have let herself be cooped up alone in her house the way April had done? Would she have let her children be strangers to keep her husband happy?

No, Ginny thought. *She wouldn't have.*

In fact, her mother would never have been deceived by someone like Ron. Not ever. Which was why April was only like her mom in some ways, and definitely not enough like her to keep Ginny from doing what needed to be done.

April looked over at Ginny, smiled, and waved. Ginny smiled and waved back. Yes, they were becoming very good friends, just the way she wanted it.

Twenty Two

Marsha parked in front of Cindy's, feeling a pinch of worry. Why in the world was she meeting Judith here? Had it ever happened before? Even when she was living in Cindy's house after moving back to Spring Falls, had anyone ever come over?

Not that she could remember. It was ParaTi's or Judith's house, and now sometimes at the Ruby House, but never at Cindy's. So something was up. But having no idea what it was made her want to go back to bed. All the months that she did just that at Cindy's flooded back to her. She'd sleep in forever, and Cindy would pretend that it was okay.

This time, it was exactly the opposite. She couldn't sleep for worrying, so instead of pacing the floor, she got in the car and got to Cindy's even before she was expected to be there. Unheard of for her.

Yes, she could have gone for a walk in the woods, done yoga, even just read a book, but her anxiety wouldn't let her. She needed to get it over with—whatever it was—as soon as possible.

Of course, it could be something good, Marsha thought, but if it was, why not meet where they usually did? Why just the three of them? No, something was up, and she could feel in her bones that it was not good. How could it be?

While Marsha fretted in her car before getting out, Cindy was upstairs in her art studio, watching from the window. She prayed that she would have the right words for Marsha. That she could be part of something good today, instead of something that tore Marsha's life apart.

During the months that Marsha lived in her house, Cindy had come to care deeply about her. Ever since Bree brought Marsha into their circle after meeting her in dance class, Marsha was always the one who did what she wanted in her own timing. It was sometimes frustrating, and there would be times she would tick them off when she would seem to stall about getting anything done.

But watching Marsha struggle and then pull herself out of the depression that overtook her when she returned to Spring Falls, Cindy understood her better and admired her courage.

While Marsha lived with her, Cindy did everything she could to support her, even though Marsha resisted most of it. There was always something private about Marsha. When they were younger, the Ruby Sisters had attributed her behavior to the fact that Marsha had a mother who couldn't be there for her because she was too busy losing herself in drink. And a completely absent father.

Cindy giggled a little. She was worried, nervous, but she was also happy. Today, they would give Marsha her father. Cindy hoped they did it in a way that gave Marsha a vision of what it would be like to spend just a little time with the man who had obviously always loved her, and then got stuck in past decisions.

Everyone knew how that could be. Cindy certainly did. She had decided she was an artist, built a successful business selling art, thinking it would support her career as an artist. Instead, she discovered she wasn't an artist at all. And now she was stuck in that past decision.

Looking around the room with all the canvases stacked face first against the wall so she didn't have to look at her failures, Cindy sighed. It was the perfect room to pretend to be something she wasn't. She had skylights installed, so she had perfect light for painting. She had all the supplies she needed. She had the time and the space.

But none of that would solve the problem of a lack of talent. She had fooled herself before. But now she knew. Still, it was her secret to keep. No one needed to know what she had learned about herself. To them, she was happy and successful and that was the way she wanted everyone to think of her.

As Cindy left the room, closing and locking the door behind her so no one would accidentally stumble into her room full of failures, she wondered if Marsha had secrets she wasn't sharing and that was why she always felt as if Marsha lived behind a closed door.

Maybe today they could at least open that door for Marsha, even if nothing could be done for her.

Although she still had a key, Marsha knocked since she didn't live there anymore. Cindy yelled, "Come in." Marsha found Cindy in the kitchen, making coffee.

"I was going to make something to eat with these, but Judith said she'd bring some of her cinnamon buns."

"And I did," Judith said, sweeping into the kitchen, holding a tray of cinnamon buns with a hot pad. "And they are just out of the oven. I rushed over here so they are still nice and warm."

"Yum," Cindy said, grabbing plates for everyone. "Let's eat in the garden."

Marsha thought it was interesting that all the Ruby Sisters had a garden. She knew Cindy hired gardeners instead of taking care of it herself the way that Bree did and Bruce said he would once his garden was set up. Marsha and April had talked about what kind of garden they wanted to have, but when April left, they put all that on hold.

Maybe we could talk about it soon, Marsha thought. It was just another thing on Marsha's list of what needed to be discussed with April. Assuming that today's meeting wouldn't change that future she was making for herself.

Cindy's garden was a walled-in private garden, which made a micro climate warm enough for them to feel comfortable around the table on the small deck outside the kitchen. When Marsha lived there, sometimes when Cindy wasn't home, she would sit at the table sipping coffee by herself, wondering what she was going to do with her life.

Now, as she noticed Cindy's nervous energy and Judith's resolve, she was terrified. They had something to say that would change her life again. Had she done something wrong? Was she just not good enough for the Ruby Sisters? Were they turning against her?

She was too terrified to move, even though she wanted to get up and leave before they left her.

Of course, it was Judith who was going to tell. She was going to right some kind of wrong by getting rid of her. Marsha watched Cindy's face to see how bad it was going to be. She knew it would be really bad when she saw Cindy's eyes fill with tears.

However, in all her years of worry and fear of what was going to happen to her, never would Marsha have thought she would hear the words that Judith spoke. Words that stopped the world as she knew it, and turned it into something else.

"Marsha, we have fantastic news for you. We know who your father is, and he wants to see you."

Twenty Three

"I'm heading out," Judith had called up the stairs to April and Ginny. Both of them had said "okay," in response. Ginny knew April was just going to pull the covers up and go back to sleep because she had told them both she was going to sleep in.

Just as well, Ginny thought. *She won't be asking me where I am going.*

When Judith called up, Ginny was already dressed. She had heard the sound of cooking in the kitchen, and soon the house smelled like the Cinnabuns she would get at the airport.

April had told her about Judith's cinnamon buns, so it delighted her when she came downstairs after Judith left to find a note beside a plate of buns that said they were for her and April.

She grabbed two, poured herself a coffee and headed to the living room, where she sunk down into the couch, and put her feet up on the coffee table. Everything about Judith's house was comfortable. She would be happy staying here for a long time.

An hour later, when April came downstairs, Ginny was still there. Reading one of Judith's books, legs still on the coffee table, and a plate full of crumbs on the couch beside her.

For a moment, April was annoyed. During all the time she lived at Judith's, she had never thought it was okay to do what Ginny was doing. To her, it felt as if Ginny was being disrespectful.

But when Ginny looked up at April and smiled, the annoyance faded. *Perhaps Ginny just doesn't know better,* April thought. But still it bothered her, and a part of her hoped that now that the birthday party was over, Ginny would move on.

Saying nothing, she took the plate off the couch, and came back a minute later with her own cinnamon bun and coffee, and set it on the coffee table, forcing Ginny to take her feet off of it.

The coward's way out, she thought to herself.

Out loud, she asked, "So, where are you heading next?"

"I think I'll stick around for a while. I see why you like this town. I'd like to get to know it and the people a little more. Maybe work at the gallery with you?"

April tried not to let the panic she felt show, as she calmly replied that she knew Cindy didn't need any more help.

"Well then, maybe I could help with the Ruby House? I don't just want to sit around doing nothing."

April calmly sipped her coffee, pretending to think about it, when all of her was screaming *no*. No, she didn't even want to work on the Ruby House herself, and she definitely didn't want Ginny working on it.

"Thanks for asking. But I'm going to let it sit for a bit. Besides, with Seth and Marsha helping me, that is enough. You know what they say about too many cooks!"

"Well, okay then. I think I'll head into town and see what's happening there. Maybe another opportunity will appear. I don't really need a job. I can just bum around for a while."

"I never asked you how you could do that. Are you independently wealthy? Or a trust fund baby?"

Although April had tried to ask casually, she could hear the undertone of distrust in her voice. Not good. Here she was, treating her friend disrespectfully. *It's Ron's fault*, April thought. I wonder if I will always be afraid of people now.

"I'm sorry, that didn't come out right. I was just curious."

Ginny leaned over and patted April's hand before saying, "Ah, no worries. It is kinda weird I can live like this. I realize how lucky I am. And it is something like that. I do have a pot of money. But eventually it will run out. But right now, I'm good. And I love having this kind of freedom. Do you want to come into town with me?"

April shook her head. "No, you go on."

What April couldn't say was that she wasn't ready to be seen in public. She was still expecting a backlash against her and although nothing like that had happened, nor would it, Judith had told her. She was still leery.

"Okay, I'll see you when I see you," Ginny said, grabbed her purse, and headed out the door.

April remained in her chair, feeling the difference in the room, looking at the crumbs on the couch, the coffee cup still on the table, and wondered who she had brought home and if it had been a good idea after all.

After cleaning up Judith's living room and kitchen, April realized she needed some advice. Not just about Ginny, but about what to do next in life. So she texted Bree, asking if she was free.

"Sure. By the time you get here, I'll have finished up the next chapter, and I'll be ready for a break."

"Be there in a few."

"Bring walking shoes and a jacket. Let's go to the falls."

An hour later, that's where they were. It had rained for a few days, so the falls were bigger than normal, crashing into the rocks spraying water everywhere. During dry spells, the falls sometimes shrunk down to just a trickle, and the spring it fed would be a dry bed.

Other times rain came down so fast it had nowhere to go, turning the area around the falls into a marsh, and then disappearing in a few days.

Today, though, it was the way they remembered in their youth. Loud, wet, and sparkling in the sunshine. Neither had talked much as they walked to the falls, both of them breathing in the scents of the small forest that surrounded the falls.

Once they were settled on the bench, Bree said, "Do you think the town is called Spring Falls because in the spring it's actually a falls?"

April laughed. "Wouldn't it be wonderful if life was that literal?"

"It would. But we know it isn't. Do you want to tell me what's bothering you?"

April sighed. "So many things, really. But mostly it's my distrust of anything ever being good again."

Bree felt her hackles rise. Deceitful and evil people who told lies because they could, who didn't care how much they hurt other people, made her want to either stop the world and get off, or fight everything wrong about it. She knew neither of those things would work. But in that moment, she wished it would.

She was also ticked at April. Didn't she see all the good staring her right in the face?

"You know that's crap, April. "

April laughed. "I knew I could count on you telling me as it is, and of course you are right. Okay, let me be more specific."

"It's that Ginny woman, isn't it?"

"Yes. I liked her. And now I am not so sure. But why? She keeps doing things that bother me. Is Ginny just unaware, or is she up to something?"

Twenty Four

G inny loved that she knew where everyone was. As soon as she settled in her seat at one of the coffee shops in town, she had checked the tracking app on her phone to find the location of all five Ruby Sisters.

She watched as April headed towards Bree and laughed to herself. *Yea right. Sure, April was just going to stay home.* She had known April was lying.

And since Judith and Marsha were still at Cindy's, that meant Cindy wasn't at the art gallery. She'd give anything to know what they were talking about, but she was sure she'd find out, eventually.

In the meantime, Ginny thought, *I'll take advantage of the situation and head over to the gallery to talk to Mimi and Janet. Maybe I'll get some scuttlebutt on the people of Spring Falls, but especially about the Ruby Sisters.*

A few minutes later, she was in her car heading towards the gallery, wondering why anyone would live in such a small town. *What do they do here?* She wondered. *No, I'm a big city girl. As soon as I get what I want, I am heading back to the city.*

What Ginny didn't know was she was also being tracked. While Cindy was hugging Marsha after their announcement, Judith had glanced at her phone and had seen Ginny heading toward the art gallery.

She is probably trying to cause some mischief, Judith thought. No, she didn't trust Ginny. And although she knew it was probably illegal to do so, she had put a tracker on Ginny's car. She'd apologize later if she got caught.

Tit for tat, she thought to herself. She had already seen the tracker on her own car, and knew it was Ginny who had put it there. And seeing it, she knew she was right about Ginny. She hadn't bought the story that Ginny had met April by chance, in the middle of nowhere, and became friendly enough that April invited her to come with her to Spring Falls.

It pleased Judith that Ginny was staying at her house. That meant that she had some control over what was going on. Between the cameras she kept around the house and office and the weekly sweep she did for listening devices—being careful that no one was listening in on her client's businesses—she knew Ginny had put trackers on all their cars.

But Judith had kept what she had found out to herself. She didn't want to alert Ginny to her suspicions. However, even before finding the trackers, she had been suspicious. A stranger had come to town claiming to be April's newfound friend? That rang alert bells for her from the moment she had heard about it.

After all, April was the wife of a man on the most-wanted list. To confirm what her gut was telling her, Judith had gone to her elusive friend Matt and asked for help. Matt, the computer guy who worked magic on the Internet, was happy for the work. Besides, Judith paid well.

But right now, Ginny was heading for the art gallery, and that worried Judith. Perhaps she needed to tell someone of her suspicions. While Cindy got up to get coffee for them and water for Marsha, Judith quickly texted Booker and asked him to stop by the office later. She'd tell him about the trackers. But she knew he would want more answers before doing anything.

He'd ask the same questions. Who was Ginny Lynn? Why was Ginny in Spring Falls? Did she deliberately make friends with April? Was she dangerous? And right now, all they had were suspicions.

Judith decided to wait until she talked to Booker and heard from Matt before talking to the Ruby Sisters. She didn't want anyone alerting Ginny before they figured out who Ginny was and what she wanted.

When Cindy brought the coffee out, Judith put her phone away. She'd deal with Ginny later. Right now, she had a friend to take care of, because Marsha had not taken the news about her father well.

Marsha had stared at Judith and Cindy and thought she must have misunderstood. Although she wanted to ask them to repeat it, she was afraid she'd hear the same thing again.

They knew her father? He loved her?

This was a ton of bull crap. No way. They were lying. Or maybe teasing. But why were they so serious? Why bring her to Cindy's to play this cruel joke on her?

While all those thoughts were rolling around in her head, Marsha was completely unaware that she had gone white and was shaking so hard her chair legs were hitting the floor. She was barely aware that Cindy had her arms around her saying something about everything was going to be okay.

But what was going to be okay? Marsha asked herself.

Then she felt Judith and Cindy help her onto the couch, and Cindy handed her a glass of water.

Both of them sat beside her as she took a sip of water.

Waiting. They are waiting for me to say something, Marsha thought.

In the background, she could hear music playing and wondered where it was coming from, and then realized it was in her own head. A song from her childhood. Why was she remembering that now?

She leaned back into the couch and closed her eyes. Her friends waited. She didn't see Cindy mouth to Judith, "Will she be okay?" and Judith nod yes.

Finally, she opened her eyes and said, "I thought you said that you know who my father is and that he wants to see me."

Cindy put her arms around Marsha as Judith answered.

"We did say that, Marsha. We met him. He wants to meet with you. He's here in Spring Falls, working with Bruce, and he asked us to set up a meeting with you."

"What? Bruce knows him? Why?"

Marsha was beginning to feel better, but only because she was getting angry. Were they working with her father behind her back?

Feeling the fight coming back into Marsha, Cindy stood and got one of her kitchen chairs and put it directly in front of Marsha. Their knees touching, she gently held Marsha's hand as she answered.

"He came to Bruce to put his affairs in order. He's dying, Marsha. This is your chance to meet him. You can be mad all you want. But you will regret not knowing why he wasn't in your life, and who he is."

Marsha stared into Cindy's blue eyes, and then looked at Judith and sighed.

"Do you two like him?"

"As much as we know about him. And Bruce calls him a friend now."

Marsha thought about kind, steady Bruce liking the man who was her father and then said.

"When would this happen?"

"Now, if you are ready."

Another wave of both fear and sorrow rushed over her. Would she ever be ready? Not really. So now was as good a time as any.

Twenty Five

Harry got the call from Judith while Amir drove him past the art gallery. Harry had wanted to see if his daughter Marsha was in there. He knew she probably wouldn't be, but every day he made a point of passing her favorite places.

Because the house she and her friend April were renovating was where Marsha was living, he had driven by there first. He knew it bordered on creepy, but he treasured the moments he saw her, even if it was only a brief glance.

Besides, he was also enjoying traveling through the town that used to be his. Long ago, when he was young and stupid. Now he felt old, and probably just as stupid.

As they drove past the blooming pear trees that lined the streets and golden patches of daffodils that cropped up almost everywhere, Harry wondered how many days he had left to enjoy the beauty of spring. His last one. He also wondered if there were seasons in the next life. He'd know soon enough.

Amir glanced in the rear-view mirror and saw the old man huddled under blankets, keeping his head turned to watch the world go by. If he could do anything to save his boss's life, he would. But this was something no one could stop.

Amir knew exactly which route to take. He knew what Harry wanted to see, always hoping to catch even a brief glance of his daughter. They had been doing this together for over a half a century. Amir was only a few years younger than Harry, but Harry was sick and he wasn't.

Amir had long ago decided that he would stay to the end, and then go home and play with his grandchildren with his patient wife, and watch the flowers grow in the garden.

So when Harry's phone rang, Amir prayed it was the call Harry had been waiting for. Harry's phone used to ring all the time with business calls. Now that his businesses had either been sold or given away, Harry's phone was quiet. The only calls Harry got these days were from his doctors—or Bruce.

Amir kept driving, noticed the woman who had come to town with April staring at the car as they went past the gallery, and wondered exactly who she was. But then Harry whispered from the back seat, "Cindy's house," and all thoughts of anything but his boss's happiness slipped from his mind.

Pulling up in front of Cindy's, he saw Bruce waiting for them. Bruce looked almost as nervous as Harry as he helped him out of the car. Judith, red hair flaming, walked down the driveway to assist.

"Would you like some coffee, something to eat?" Judith asked Amir.

Amir smiled and pointed to the seat beside him and a battered lunch box.

"I always make sure to bring food and coffee. But thank you."

Judith reached in and held Amir's hand that she could see trembling on the steering wheel.

"He'll be okay. We'll take care of him in there."

Amir nodded. He trusted these women. Even so, Harry and his daughter together was either a powder keg that could destroy, or a gift, and he was afraid that it would be the powder keg.

Judith handed Amir her card. "Whatever you need, Amir."

As Amir watched Judith head back to the house, he thought about what he had heard about her. A fighter, always making things right. But what he didn't always hear about was her kind heart.

Yes. Harry was in excellent hands. Now all he could do was wait and pray.

Ginny stood inside of the art gallery looking out the front window, waiting for Mimi and Janet to come out of the gallery office, and wondered who was in the black car that went by. She thought she had seen it earlier, cruising the streets. A driver and a passenger. How unlikely was it that someone like that would be in Spring Falls?

Was it a developer looking to buy property? Why, she didn't know. But just because she didn't like small towns didn't mean others didn't. Still, that didn't seem like the answer.

The only other thing the town had going for it was its community college. *Or perhaps it's about April's husband,* Ginny thought. *After all, that's the story here, isn't it?*

Maybe she'd ask Janet and Mimi if they knew who it was. Otherwise, she'd have to do some research on her own. She wasn't about ready to give up her position within the Ruby Sisters circle, and if, by chance, whomever was in that car would upset her plans, she'd have to stop them.

Janet stood in the office door, watching Ginny stare out the window at something. Mimi stepped up beside her and whispered, "Do you trust her?"

"Not for a second. But I don't know why. What do you think she's up to?"

Before Janet answered, Ginny turned, all smiles, and asked, "Got a minute to chat now?"

"Sure." Mimi answered, "But let's talk in the office. Because I only have a few minutes."

Ginny kept a smile on her face, even though she was disappointed. Only a few minutes? It would have to be enough.

Following Mimi, she asked, "Have you seen that black car with a driver cruising around town? Do you know what's that about?"

"Nope, haven't, so no idea."

Over Ginny's head, Mimi winked at Janet. She had lied about the first, but not the second. They had seen the car, but no, they didn't know who it was.

They both hoped it was something good. In the meantime, although Ginny thought she was going to get something out of them, first they planned on learning something about her.

So Mimi's first question to Ginny as she settled into her chair was, "So, tell us about yourself? What did you do before you met April? What are your plans?"

Ginny kept a smile on her face and prepared to give her the same story she gave April. But inside, a tremor of worry had begun. Who were these people? Maybe they weren't as dumb as she thought they were.

Still, she was smarter. And she'd get what she wanted, and be out of town before they knew what hit them.

Twenty Six

When Judith stepped out of the front door to greet Harry, Marsha thought about running out the back door. She hadn't known her father her whole life. Why start now?

Instead, she told herself to put her big girl pants on, and watched from the window as Bruce helped an old man out of the car, and Judith spoke to the driver.

A driver. Her father had a driver. And she had seen that car cruising by the Ruby House. Judith had told her that her father had been watching over her for years, but she didn't know how close he was and what that meant until she realized he had been in that car. How creepy was that? Why didn't he just let her know who he was? What did he have to hide? Why did he leave?

All the questions she had banged around inside her head like irritating mosquitoes that wouldn't leave her alone. With her hands clenched at her side, she watched Bruce help the old man up the driveway. While she watched, Marsha fully realized how furious she had been her whole life that she never had a father. And now that he was here, that fury felt all-consuming. But instead of the anger strengthening her, she felt as if she was shriveling up inside. The mood she often spoke of as a dark cloud that enveloped her loomed close by.

Cindy stood beside her as she watched.

"You can do this, Marsha. Not everyone gets this kind of chance."

As Cindy spoke, the dark cloud moved a little further away, but Marsha knew it was waiting for a chance to move in and she wasn't so sure she actually wanted to stop it. It might be better than the fire she felt now.

Marsha nodded, wanting to be grateful for Cindy's words, but not so sure this was the kind of chance she wanted. Most people got a chance to actually grow up with a father. That was something she would never have.

But even as she thought that, she knew it wasn't true. Many people had a far worse childhood than she did. By the time the old man walked through the door, Marsha had talked herself into being polite and was holding off the dark mood—for now. She remained standing by the window while Bruce settled the man, who said he was her father, into a chair, and wrapped a blanket around his legs.

Even from where she was standing, Marsha could see that he was trembling. Was it because of his sickness or because he was afraid?

And as hard on him as Marsha wanted to be, and as much as she wanted to tell him to go away, she found she couldn't. Yes, she was still angry. He had deserted her, but now she wanted to know why.

"Can I get anything for anyone?" Cindy asked.

"Sure," Judith said, tilting her head at Bruce and walking towards the kitchen. "Perhaps we can help you?"

Bruce took the hint, put his hand on Harry's shoulder and left the room with Cindy and Judith, leaving Harry and Marsha to stare at each other. Bruce wondered which one of them would speak first.

It was Harry. "I am sorry. I know it is not enough to say how sorry I am that I robbed you of a childhood with a father that loved you. But I did love you. And I have always been here for you. Even though you didn't know me, I knew you."

Marsha said nothing. Waiting. She knew she was waiting for the why. Why would a man who claimed to love his child leave her?

When Harry tried to say more, he started coughing, and couldn't speak. Without thinking, Marsha stood and handed him the water Cindy had left on the table beside him. His hands were shaking so hard she had to help him lift the glass, and as he looked up to thank her, she realized she had his gray eyes.

Until that moment, she wanted to doubt that this man was her father, but now she knew. He was.

So when she sat back down, she asked the question. "Why? Why did you leave? If you were always around, why didn't you let me know?"

Harry paused, his hands trembling, and shook his head, unshed tears in his eyes. But Marsha didn't care. Her heart felt like a stone and even though she wanted to know why he had left, she was sure nothing he said would make her care about him.

"Your mother forbade me, and when she first did, I understood why. I thought she was right. When I finally came to my senses and realized the mistake I had made, it seemed too late. I was afraid you'd hate me. So instead I made up a fantasy world, where you and I talked.

"I watched you grow up from a distance. We had some lovely conversations. And of course, I was busy building businesses. Rationalization is a powerful thing. And it seemed logical to me to let you live your life on your own.

"You were doing well. Or so I told myself. And then I got sick."

Seeing Marsha's stony face, he added, "I am not making excuses. I have no excuses. You asked why, and that was why. And I don't expect you to forgive me. You have already given me so much just by sitting here in this room with me."

After another bout of coughing and waving off Bruce, who had come into the room to see if he was okay, Harry leaned back into the chair and waited.

Marsha waited, too. She waited to see how she felt. She waited to see if anything had changed. The black cloud moved a little further away.

"How sick are you? And what do you have? Cancer?"

"Very. I was supposed to die months ago. But I am a stubborn old man. I was determined to tell you the truth first. And no, I don't have cancer. I have many things wrong with me. Everything is shutting down, as my doctors have told me. All a result of having AIDS."

Marsha turned pale. She felt as if she was going to throw up. It couldn't be. Her father had AIDS.

"How, from a needle, blood transfusion?"

"No. From being a young and foolish gay man."

Although Marsha felt the words as a blow, she had to ask again before she lost the courage and will to ask. "But why did you agree to not be in my life?"

"I thought I was doing the right thing. It was a different time then. It's a little better now. Some countries still kill what they call the gays. But then, it was terrible. We lived in fear. People hated us. Your mother, like many people, believed us to be evil.

"Did you know that when the 1973 fire happened in the UpStairs Lounge in New Orleans, and killed thirty-two people, some families didn't even come forward to claim the bodies of the victims? It was because it was a gay bar.

"It was a horrible time, Marsha. Your mother was afraid for you. She was angry at me. She was trying to protect you. We both were."

Harry started coughing again, but Marsha didn't move to help him. He had just turned her entire world upside down, and now she did not know what to do. So she got up and walked out the door, letting it slam behind her.

Twenty Seven

While Harry tried to explain himself to Marsha, and while Ginny, Mimi, and Janet talked at the gallery, April and Bree were still sitting on the bench on the path to the falls.

Beside the path, swaths of pink, purple, and yellow crocuses showed through the leaves on the forest floor. A whole patch of ferns were uncurling, surrounded by patches of trillium, bloodroot, Dutchman's breeches, and Virginia bluebells.

The trees had leafed out into multiple shades of green that would turn to dark green in the summer, but right now looked like fall in reverse. Further into the woods, they could see a blooming wild cherry, its pink and white flowers lit by a shaft of sunlight. Near the bench, an apple tree bloomed. A petal drifted in the cool wind, landing in April's hair.

Drops of water left over from the rain fell to the ground as birds flew through the trees, and the wind moved the branches. Masses of different kinds of mushrooms were growing everywhere, and squirrels rushed through the leaves, looking for the nuts they had buried in the fall. Bree thought it looked like a fairy wonderland.

"I can't ever decide if I like fall or spring best," Bree said. "This is so beautiful, it almost seems impossible that it exists."

"I know what you mean. It's indescribably beautiful. I guess it's whichever season we are in at the moment that seems the most beautiful," April answered, brushing the petal out of her hair and shivering a little, but not enough to make her want to move.

However, April was glad that Bree reminded her to dress warmly and wear walking shoes, not sneakers. The path was muddy, and sometimes the breeze was chilly.

With the falls roaring in the distance, they had stayed on the bench, neither of them wanting to go somewhere else. Spring came and went so quickly, they didn't want to waste a minute.

After a few moments of taking in the day's beauty, April and Bree continued their conversation about Ginny. They had already agreed that they didn't trust her, but they didn't know why. She was pushy and rude, but did that make her untrustworthy?

"Has Booker met her yet?" April asked.

"Don't know. We should probably bring him into it, if Judith hasn't already."

April said nothing more, waiting. Bree was fully aware of what April wanted next. She wanted to know more about her and Booker.

"We are just friends."

"Hum. Friends. There are many kinds of friends. After all, we've been friends since second grade."

"Seems impossible, doesn't it? We were cuter then though," Bree said, thinking about the day she met April with her bubbling radiant energy, fluffy brown hair that reminded them all of feathers, and blue eyes. April still had her blue eyes and hair that looked like wings, even though it was much grayer. But April's boundless radiant energy was not there anymore.

"We were," April agreed, and then asked, "Would we have made the same choices we made back then if we had known what it would lead to?"

"It's something I think about once in a while. I would have told my secret sooner, but in the end, it worked out. And even if I had known that Paul would die and leave me, I'd still have married him. He was my one and only, if there is such a thing."

"I'm not sure if I would," April said after a long pause. Bree took her friend's hand and held it for a moment, understanding that it was too soon for April to know. Her pain was still front and center.

"The question probably is," Bree said, "If we could look back thirty years from now to this moment in time, and knew the outcome of the choices we were making now, would we make them?

"We are both in transition, from the life we used to know to the one we are living in now, although I have a few months more behind me than you do. But we both lost our husbands, and have new choices to make."

"The problem is, Bree, I don't know what choices are in front of me. Every day is just a step forward, trying not to look backward. Trying not to think about the life Ron has left me with, a legacy that my children and I might never recover from.

"Your husband left by dying. But on the way out, he did everything he could to make sure your life without him would be full and happy. After all, here we all are together again, and without him, that might never have happened.

"You even got his blessing to move on with your life with Booker, if that is what you want."

For a moment, both of them thought of that moment when holding on to Bryan Anderson's arm, they had all watched Paul step into the light.

"But me, I still have a husband out there somewhere. A man who claimed to love me, but never actually claimed to love his children, if I am going to be truthful about it. A man who raped and killed countless women. Until, and if they catch him, we'll never know how many. Maybe not even then.

"You were living with a good man, and I was living with an evil one, and I didn't even know him. I want Ron gone. I want the story of that life erased forever. You want to treasure your past. I want it to never have happened.

"So I think the question means different things to each of us. You have only a few decisions to make, but no matter what you decide, you will be happy and safe.

"I don't know if I will ever be safe, or truly happy. I probably haven't been that kind of deep-hearted happy since the moment I met Ron. That I misjudged his love, my happiness, all of our life together is terrifying. How could I know if what I have to decide now is going to be good, or worth anything at all?"

Bree knew enough not to ask, "But what about your children, or us, your friends, or the business you want to build?" April didn't want to be fixed. She wanted to be heard and understood.

So even though Bree wasn't a hugger, she reached out and pulled April in close and said, "You're right. But I know I choose to be your friend forever, whatever that takes."

Speechless, April turned her head and cried into Bree's shoulder.

Twenty Eight

Judith heard the door slam and rushed into the living room, just in time to see Marsha pull away from the curb, tires squealing, almost running into the curb on the other side of the street.

Behind her, Harry couldn't stop coughing.

Amir, having seen Marsha run out of the house, knew what had happened, and terrified for his employer, ran for the house, leaving the door of the car open in his haste, something he had never done in all the years he had worked for Harry.

It was as he had feared. Marsha had rejected her father, and although he understood why she might feel that way, Amir was furious at her. Couldn't Marsha see Harry thought he had done the right thing?

And even if she couldn't, couldn't she find some love in her heart for a dying man? *Apparently not*, Amir thought.

And then all worries about Marsha and what she thought vanished as he reached the door and heard Judith calling for an ambulance.

"I can get him there quicker," Amir said. "And there is oxygen in the car."

Judith nodded, still on the phone, canceled the ambulance but asked them to alert the hospital.

Bruce and Amir lifted Harry and rushed him to the car. Bruce sat in the back seat, Harry's head on his lap, holding an oxygen mask on his face, and Amir pealed away from the curb even faster than Marsha had done, the directions to the hospital burned into his brain.

Amir knew this moment would happen. He thought he was prepared. But seeing Harry slumped over, he knew he wasn't. Probably never would be. Amir hoped Harry had gotten some peace from the telling, but looking at him lying gray and still on Bruce's lap, his long legs dangling off the seat, Amir feared that had not happened.

If he hadn't learned how to contain his emotions over the years, Amir would have pounded the steering wheel and screamed at the world. But he couldn't. Wouldn't. He wouldn't give into the fear. He'd get Harry to the hospital alive, and then he could break down privately.

He'd call his wife, and his silence on the phone would tell her everything she needed to know. And she would be there for him when he got home, as she always had been.

From the window, Judith could see Amir's face, a mask of determination. She hadn't realized until that moment that Amir loved Harry. She wondered if Harry knew that.

Cindy stood beside Judith, watching them drive away, the two of them holding hands, both of them with tears running down their cheeks.

Not just for Harry, but for Marsha. For Harry for what he knew he had lost, and for Marsha because she never had it.

"I'll go find Marsha while you go to the hospital. Let me know how he is."

Judith nodded, grabbed her messenger bag filled with everything she would need wherever she went, and headed to the door. Then she turned around and hugged Cindy.

Cindy didn't need to ask why. She felt the same way. They had each other. It was a gift they would never take for granted.

Now she had to find Marsha. And bring her back to them, and if Harry lived through this, back to him. Not so much for Harry, although she wanted that for him, too. but for Marsha, who would never forgive herself if she left it this way. It might take years, but it would eat away at her and she would never be the same.

Not on my watch, Cindy said to herself. *Now where would Marsha go?*

Marsha wasn't thinking at all. She was angry. She was sad. No, she was furious. Disgusted. Afraid. All the things she was feeling all at once turned everything she was doing into a blur. She felt alone. Abandoned. Everyone had failed her.

She had no idea where to go or what to do. All she knew was she had to get away. Maybe go back to the Ruby House and grab a few things and run. Go somewhere else. Anywhere else.

But as much as Marsha wanted to run away and never return, the tiny rational piece of her brain that was still working told her that would never work.

When she almost hit the curb, pulling away from the house, she made herself so afraid that she could feel her insides trembling. Even her teeth were chattering. Not because she was cold. Just afraid, and she knew who she was afraid of. She was afraid of herself. Afraid of what she might do. Afraid of who she was and told no one.

And now her father dangled it out in front of her, and look what it had gotten him. A life being a creepy stranger to his own daughter.

Marsha drove, not knowing where she was going, and was surprised to find herself in the parking lot that led to the falls.

Well, maybe I do have a little common sense, Marsha said to herself. *I got myself to a safe place. And a walk in the woods is something Bree swears makes things better.*

Reaching behind the seat, Marsha grabbed her hat, jammed it onto her head, took a deep breath, and stepped out of the car. She heard a crow call in the distance, one of the few birds she recognized. For some reason, it calmed her. Bree had told her crows lived in communities and cared about each other.

"No matter what?" Marsha had asked Bree. Bree had paused a moment, and Marsha had wondered why. Wondering if she was thinking how the Ruby Sisters had accepted her even after telling them her secret about Ron being Mary's father.

"Yes, I believe it would be no matter what," Bree had eventually answered.

Keeping her head down, Marsha stepped onto the path, breathing in the spring smells, and stood listening to the bird songs she didn't recognize. And realized she already felt better.

Maybe a walk to the falls was just what I need, Marsha thought. *I won't think about anything at all, just breathe and listen.*

Which is what she did, so by the time she reached the bench, she felt marginally better. And when she saw her two friends sitting on the bench as if they were waiting for her, she figured the crow was telling her something after all.

"Go to your friends," the crow had said. And then, here they were. And whatever she told them, they would understand. Or so she hoped. But she was ready to try it out.

Bree and April looked up in surprise and delight at seeing Marsha, but seeing her face, April said, "What's wrong?"

"I'll tell you," Cindy said, gasping as she stumbled up the path right behind Marsha.

"Wait? What are you doing here? Did you follow me?" Marsha asked, staring at her friend, who was leaning over, hands on her knees, trying to get her breath.

"Lucky guess," she said.

"What's going on?" Bree demanded, hands on her hips. "And since we are all here, where's Judith?"

"At the hospital with Marsha's father."

Bree and April stared at Cindy as if she had grown a second head, as Marsha burst into tears.

"It's a long story," Cindy said, hugging Marsha.

In the branches overhead, a murder of crows watched. Silent. As if they understood.

Twenty Nine

On the way to the hospital, Judith called her assistant and canceled her afternoon appointments, Then she asked her to contact Booker and have him meet her at the hospital.

"Tell him it's for a client."

"Okay," Nancy replied. "But you also got a call from Nicky. Do you want to call her or have me tell her you're busy?"

"Did she say what she wanted?"

"No."

"Okay, I'll call her."

Judith's mind was racing. What could Nicky want? And did she have time for it, whatever it was? But she owed her. It was because of Nicky and her search for her sister Sara that the truth about Ron had come out. Or course it had thrown April's life into a tailspin, one which they were all just coming out of.

Judith sighed. And then Harry came to town and upset everything again. She wondered what was next, and then chuckled to herself. *Admit it, you love this mystery solving. Figuring things out, finding solutions, even the drama of it.*

Sometimes it bothered Judith that she was this way. Was it weird to get pleasure when things went wrong so she could fix them? And when it was at the expense of her friends, it didn't seem right.

But then she heard the little voice in her gut that she had come to trust remind her that she didn't cause the problems. The pleasure she got from the problems was from being part of the solution.

Yes, that's it, Judith said to herself. *That's where the pleasure lies.*

By the time Judith reached the hospital she was ready to do whatever it took to have Harry and Marsha be together. That is if Harry was still alive. So when the receptionist at the hospital saw her, recognizing her from town meetings, she gave up Harry's room number without a fight.

Judith didn't bother asking how he was. He had a room. He was still alive. Breathing a *thank you* to whomever was listening, she headed to Harry's room, unaware her red hair was flaming and that she was talking to herself.

Nicky put the phone down and turned to her sister.

"She wasn't there."

"So you are going, anyway?"

"Yes. I have to."

As she answered, Nicky stared at her sister, thinking how much they had both changed since finding each other again after all these years, and especially these last few months. After their tearful reunion in Booker's office, they returned to Jakestown because they both figured they had some healing to do.

They had agreed that returning to where it started was the best place to begin again. Both of them were ready to help convict Ron if they ever found him. But neither of them thought he would be. So they put his story on the back burner and concentrated on facing the past, getting to know each other again, and getting healthy.

They had moved into a small house a block away from downtown. At first, they only told Patty and John that they were in town. They talked, cried, and when they felt a little better, Patty asked them to come help her at the diner.

At first, they refused. They would be the talk of the town and they were both used to hiding away from people.

"That's the point," Patty had said. "You two need to heal, but so does the town. Seeing you will help the town recover. Then everyone can stop suspecting that it was one of us."

They had reluctantly agreed. For Patty and John, and for the town. All of them had suffered almost as much as they had. But it had taken time for the town to accept them again. Mostly because no one knew what to say. Was "I'm sorry" enough?

But soon happiness for the two sisters as they walked down the street together brought a smile to everyone who saw them. And a few months later, business at the diner had picked up as people came in to gawk, and then to talk.

Nicky had teased Patty that their working there was simply a marketing idea on her part. She had laughed and said, of course, it was. But she also needed more help. Her husband, John, was ready to retire from his position as cook.

So Sara, who had worked in restaurants for years using the name Jane Roam, started replacing John in the kitchen. Now, although people still gawked and often asked embarrassing questions, they also came to the diner to eat, having heard about Sara's cooking.

Sara still made John's famous hamburgers, but she had added other things to the menu. She added kid friendly items and even a few vegetarian dishes, which John had vetoed at first, but then agreed to try them out. And then, after tasting them, he agreed to serve them. Still, he and Patty were astonished by how many people came asking for the vegetarian items.

Both Sara and Nicky had gained some weight, so they didn't look like scrawny cats, as Patty had called them. Nicky had let her dyed hair grow out, and then cut it so now she had a halo of white hair, which everyone loved, and Nicky was getting used to. Sara had already had a cap of dark gray hair, so they teased each other about no longer being the blond sisters. Now they were the gray old sisters.

Both of them were feeling at home again in Jakestown. Patty had been right. Now that the town knew it was none of them who had done something to Sara, people smiled at each other again as they passed on the streets and returned to sitting on their porches and waved to passersby.

Every time Nicky looked at her town, it reminded her how Ron Page had done more than rape Sara. He had destroyed lives. But now they were taking theirs back.

Before Nicky and Sara had left Spring Falls, they told Booker and Judith that if there was anything they could do to catch Ron, they would do it. They had promised to keep in touch. So when April returned to Spring Falls, Judith had called Nicky to let her know.

At the time, Nicky had just said, "Okay, thanks for letting me know," chatted for a bit about what was going on with her and Sara, and hung up. It wasn't until that night, lying in bed listening to the old house creaking, that Nicky realized she had unfinished business in Spring Falls. She had to talk to April.

Even though she knew none of the Ruby Sisters blamed her, she blamed herself for destroying April's life. Nicky knew it was irrational to think that way, but still she had to do it.

Which is why she said to her sister, "I have to talk to April face to face. I need to see for myself that she is okay."

"Do you want me to go with you?" Sara asked.

"No. I have to do this myself. You stay and cook up a storm. I won't be gone long."

Sara knew she could do nothing to stop her sister from going, and she understood why, but she hoped it didn't make things worse. And although she didn't know why, Sara was worried for Nicky and what she would find in Spring Falls. Years of living on the edge had made Sara aware of things other people might not notice.

Sara hoped she was wrong. But she was afraid that she wasn't.

"Come back to me safe and sound," she said as she hugged Nicky goodbye, and then prayed to whatever gods were listening to take care of her sister.

Thirty

The drive to Spring Falls from Jakestown took a few hours, but for Nicky, it flew by. In fact, she barely remembered driving. Once in a while she glimpsed the greening trees, but mostly, she drove through the winding back roads without being consciously present.

Nicky thought back to the last time she had gone to Spring Falls, ready to do battle, get revenge, and do whatever she needed to do to stop Ron Page. She had told herself she didn't care who she hurt in the telling of her secret.

The pain she had been carrying around for years filled every pore in her body and she had no room for pity or sympathy for anyone. Including herself. But that was before she met the Ruby Sisters. After that, things were different.

The pain grew worse, because she knew she was the avenging angel bringing news that would destroy their lives. And although she had turned their lives inside out, she had destroyed no one's life, except maybe April's, and that was what she had to find out. Did April really survive?

It was still astonishing to Nicky that the Ruby Sisters had not turned against her, the messenger, or each other. Instead, they had gathered together and supported one another. But the most shocking outcome to Nicky was that instead of hating her, the Ruby Sisters had embraced her.

And it was because of their support that she and Sara had healed so quickly. Nicky knew they would never fully recover from their ordeal. But now the pain didn't take up all the space in her body and spirit. Now she had room for other things. Like going to see April and making sure she was okay.

Nicky knew it was foolish to be worrying. April was well taken care of, but still the niggle of worry persisted, and that meant she had to find out why. She had to assure herself that all was well with April and the other four Ruby Sisters.

On the way into town, Nicky drove by April's house. It seemed like it had been a lifetime ago when April had asked her to be part of its renovation. She wondered what had happened to it once April left town.

The maple tree out front blocked some of the view, but she could see a new driveway leading to what looked like a parking lot on the side of the house.

Marsha must have kept on working on it, she thought. Thinking of the run-down house where they lived, Nicky wondered if she and Sara should buy a house and have April design it.

As if we have money to do that, Nicky muttered to herself. She and Sara only made enough money to get by, not get a house and renovate it.

Nicky's plan was to go see Judith first, but as she pulled into town, she changed her mind and parked near the art gallery. She knew Janet and Mimi would be there and it would be fun to catch up with them. Besides, they had promised to give her a makeover the same way they had made over April when she first came to town, and she wanted to see what they said about how she looked now.

Parking a few doors down from the art gallery, Nicky stood for a moment looking at the town. Without the lens of fear and worry, it was even more beautiful than she remembered.

As she walked past the window of the art gallery, she was relieved to see it was as beautiful as ever, the corners and center of the gallery filled with bouquets of spring flowers. As soon as Nicky opened the door, the tingling bell announcing her arrival, Janet came into the gallery and said, "Hello, can I help you?"

Nicky smiled. It was a good sign that Janet didn't recognize her.

"OMG, Nicky," Janet squealed, practically knocking her over as she embraced her.

Mimi rushed out of the back room, worried that something had happened. A moment passed before she too recognized the woman that Janet was hugging.

"Nicky, you look fantastic!" Mimi said, joining in the hug.

And then Nicky surprised them all by bursting into tears.

A few minutes later, after wiping her eyes and sipping the water Janet had brought her, Nicky managed to say, "Thank you."

"What brings you to town?" Mimi asked. "And can you stay a while?"

"April. And I don't know."

Janet and Mimi nodded.

"We are so glad to have her home," Janet said. "And she brought a friend with her."

"A friend?"

"Someone that she met on the road, and they became travel buddies. Honestly, we are not sure why. And as much as we don't like saying it, we are not fans."

Mimi nodded in agreement, adding, "It seems harsh to say that, though. She is just a little rude. She was here earlier, and it was obvious she was picking our brain."

"About what?" Nicky asked, feeling a familiar ball of fear form inside her stomach.

"About everything. From the town, to the Ruby Sisters, to April's story. We didn't tell her much, though, and she left fairly quickly. She also asked about the black car that seems to be everywhere the past few weeks.

"She wanted to know if we knew who it was. But, we don't. I think she got bored with us since Cindy wasn't here because she had some meeting with Judith."

As Janet rambled on, Mimi glanced over at Nicky, who had turned pale and was clutching her water glass as if it was a lifeline.

"Are you okay, Nicky?"

Nicky nodded. "I don't know what's wrong. But when you said April met a stranger on the road, I felt the same thing I used to feel when I was looking for Ron."

"What could Ginny have to do with Ron?" Janet asked.

"Maybe nothing. Maybe it's just a left over fear from the last time I was here. But I want to see April. And talk to Judith. I called her and she wasn't in her office.

At that moment, Nicky's phone rang. "Speaking of Judith."

"Sorry that I didn't get right back to you," Judith said. "I'm at the hospital helping a friend. What can I do for you? In fact, why not come for a visit? You can stay at my house and we'll catch up."

"I would love that. And I am already here. At the gallery with Janet and Mimi."

"Is something wrong? Is that why you are already here?"

"I didn't think so. I was just coming to see April and make sure she was doing well. But now, I'm not so sure."

Standing in the doorway of Harry's room, Judith agreed with Nicky. Something was wrong. But what was it?

"I'm heading to my office. Could you meet me there?"

Nicky agreed and told Mimi and Janet she was heading out to meet Judith.

"What aren't you so sure about, Nicky?" Mimi asked.

Nicky shook her head. "Something doesn't feel right."

Janet and Mimi watched Nicky as she headed to Judith's office. Janet turned to Mimi and said, "See, I told you something is going on. And it's not just that black car."

Mimi nodded. She agreed with them both. But what could they do?

Thirty One

"What are you talking about?" Bree asked after Cindy said that Marsha's father was in the hospital. They were all still congregated around the bench by the falls, Cindy trying to catch her breath, Bree still standing with her hands on her hips, and April looking at all of them like they were bringing her another piece of news she couldn't handle.

They had all waited impatiently until Marsha's tears stopped, but because Marsha looked as if she was going to run at any moment, Cindy had a firm grip on her hand. It still amazed her that she had gone to the right place and found Marsha in the woods, let alone also found April and Bree. Luck was on her side then, but would it be again? Cindy would not let go of Marsha until she was sure she would stay and let them all help her.

Marsha shook her head and pointed at Cindy. Everyone knew she meant she wouldn't be doing the telling. It had to be Cindy. Cindy smiled and nodded.

"Shall we go someplace else to hear this story?" April asked.

She thought Marsha looked almost as bad as she had felt when she found out about Ron. Perhaps Marsha needed some place more comfortable to reveal whatever this was.

Marsha shook her head no, and waving her hand around in a circle, whispered, "Let's get it over with."

"Are you sure you want me to tell?" Cindy asked, wanting to be the one to tell the story, but also wanting to give Marsha a chance to tell it her way.

But Marsha just stared down at the ground, the toes of her shoes digging into the dirt by their feet. In the distance Cindy heard the rumble of passing cars and voices coming towards them, heading towards the falls. A twig snapped, and she saw a deer watching them from a distance. Cindy had the fleeting thought that Marsha's father had been like the deer. Was it a bad thing? She took a deep breath and told them all a short version of the Marsha and her dad story.

"Wait. Your father has been in the black car that has been cruising around Spring Falls?" April asked, momentarily forgetting to berate herself for being so stupid about Ron.

It was Cindy who answered. Marsha still stared at the ground as if she was wishing it would open up and swallow her.

"Yes. That's who it is. Turns out he has been around all this time. Not always in Spring Falls, but he has always been near Marsha wherever she has lived."

"Even when we were kids?" Bree asked, trying to remember if they had ever seen him.

"Even then. And yes, we probably all saw him when he attended shows and graduations. It's just that none of us knew who he was. Especially Marsha. And if Marsha's mom knew what he was doing, she never let on."

The crows above them still sat watching, which Bree thought was both lovely and slightly unnerving. Did the crows understand what was going on? Did crows have this kind of problem? What did the crows want her to do now?

"Ask the question," Bree heard. Probably not the crows, just her blunt, demanding self, wanting and needing the entire story.

Turning to Marsha, she said, "So, Harry—your father, for heaven's sake—collapsed after Marsha stormed off and Judith and Bruce took him to the hospital? Sorry, Marsha, for asking, but don't you want to know if he is still alive?"

"Isn't that a little harsh, Bree?" Cindy whispered.

"No. She's right. I should care. So, is he?"

"Judith just texted me that he is," Cindy answered. "Still alive anyway. She left Bruce there and asked us to meet her at her office."

A few minutes later, Marsha, supported by Cindy, and April and Bree following close behind, reached the parking lot. Not wanting to chance Marsha being by herself, Cindy told her they'd get her car later, and buckled her into the front seat of her car.

Once they were on the road, she asked, "Do you want to talk about it?"

Marsha just turned her head and stared out the window.

Well, this should be fun, Cindy thought. And then realized that it was fun. Not in a jump up and down sort of way, but in a useful way. That was it. She felt useful. She had something to do, something to think about other than herself and her inability to create any kind of art that meant anything.

And then there's April, she reminded herself. *And that weird woman she brought with her.* Cindy wondered if anyone else thought of her that way. Were they all being too polite? Isn't that how they all got into trouble before?

When does being polite and nice go too far? Cindy wondered. And was it wrong for her to feel more alive now that she had Marsha to help again?

Probably, she answered herself, but she was going to put off that soul searching for a while.

Still leaning against the window, her head turned away, Marsha said. "What's up with that friend of April's?"

"Seriously?" Cindy said, laughing. "That's what's on your mind?"

Marsha looked over at Cindy and they laughed together, tears still on Marsha's face, feeling marginally better. She had decided that the whole thing was pretty crazy. After all, she had just found out she had a father who, for her entire life, had stalked her, and now all she wanted to know was who was April's friend.

Deflection and distraction is what it's called, she thought. *But for now, it works for me.*

Thirty Two

*W*ell, *that was a bust,* Ginny thought as she turned off her phone recording. Sure, it was wrong to record people without their knowledge, but what did she care? And it was so easy. Anybody could be doing it at any time.

But it had been a useless thing to do. Nothing Mimi and Janet said meant a thing. She hadn't realized how easily they had led her around by the nose until she listened to the recording. Here she thought she was doing a world class job of spying, but she had been easily out-maneuvered. And that kind of pissed her off.

I might as well just erase the whole thing. Ginny thought. Because as hard as she had tried, she couldn't get anything out of Mimi and Janet other than a little local color. *Which will come in handy to fill out the story,* she realized, before pressing the delete button.

Still, it wasn't what she wanted. She wanted information only the Ruby Sisters and their friends could give her. And they weren't giving up a thing. It was as if they had all agreed to never, ever, talk about what had happened. Or even what was happening now? And there was that black car. What did it have to do with the Ruby Sisters? Because she was sure that it did.

Ginny was sure if she had more time, she could get exactly what she needed and so much more. She could take care of what she came for while getting something she hadn't expected—the black car story. It would be just for her use. She was sure there was money in there somewhere. Someone sneaking around like that had something to hide.

But time was running out. She had more than one deadline, and one of them wouldn't wait. It would be a true *dead* line for her if she failed. She couldn't and wouldn't. Nevertheless, so far she had nothing, except a story about friendship, which is not the story she had to get.

And I thought I planned this so well, Ginny thought. *Better than I ever planned before.* Well, she had. After all, here she was in Spring Falls and knew where every one of them was at all times. That was something.

She had to stop being so hard on herself. She was okay. She'd just have to be a little smarter. Pushing didn't seem to work. She'd have to resort to more subtle means. It wouldn't be that hard. After all, she was here in town, where it was all taking place. Not only was she in town, she was living in the queen bee's house, along with the fly she was catching in her web.

It will be fine, she assured herself. Had to. No one was doing it for her. Ginny had to admit that part of her upset was watching friendship at work. This was something she had never had. Ever. And she didn't expect to either. *So what,* she said to herself. She was doing just fine on her own.

Checking her phone, Ginny looked to see if Judith was still at the hospital, and saw that she was heading back to town. That had been an interesting development. Did something happen at Cindy's? Were they okay? Did Judith know someone at the hospital? Maybe she'd head over there and snoop around to see what she could learn.

On her phone, Ginny had watched Cindy and Marsha head towards Bree and April in the woods. Now they were all heading back to town. Except Marsha. Did they leave her there? Why would she be in the woods in the first place? What was going on?

The coffee and pastry had filled Ginny up for a time, but now she was hungry. She thought she'd invite April to lunch and maybe that way she could find out what was happening.

But April answered, "Sorry. Busy with the Ruby Sisters."

Well, Ginny thought. *At least she's not lying.* A few minutes later, she realized they were all going to Judith's office. Except Marsha. Where was Marsha?

Since she was still in her car, parked near the art gallery, Ginny thought about driving out to the woods to find Marsha, but decided against it. What would she accomplish there? Marsha would never talk without the other Ruby Sisters around, anyway.

Picking at the skin around her thumb, Ginny debated what to do next. She didn't like this small town. They were too friendly. People actually smiled at her as she sat in the car. How could she ever do things in secret if everyone knew everyone and paid attention to what was going on?

Well, they didn't pay attention to Ron, did they? Ginny muttered to herself. She had to do something. Learn something that she could share. But with most of the Ruby Sisters together, Marsha in the woods, and the Bruce guy at the hospital, who else could she talk to?

Wait, Ginny said to herself. *There are other people I can talk to, and kill two birds with one stone.* Or three birds. Because if Ron's daughter, the one he hadn't known about, was working at Para Ti's, Ginny thought she'd put a tracker on her car while getting some lunch. And perhaps try to get into her house afterward and see what she could find.

She had already tried Judith's home office and was not pleasantly surprised to find the door locked. Who locked their home office? Apparently paranoid Judith.

April had told Ginny that Judith was super cautious because of Ron and had installed more cameras outside the house and a few hidden ones in the house.

"So don't try anything funny," April had said, laughing.

Ginny almost swallowed her tongue when she heard that and then covered her shock by laughing, too. She wasn't sure how successful she had been though because April had momentarily squinted her eyes, and then laughed again as if she hadn't noticed Ginny's reaction.

All the more reason to get this done, and get out of here, Ginny thought, heading to ParaTi's.

Thirty Three

*H*e looks like a moth pinned against the bed, Bruce thought, watching Harry with all the tubes sticking out of him. Amir had stepped out to get him coffee, saying he would stay and watch, and Bruce could leave.

But he couldn't. He had never seen someone collapse before. Of course, in Harry's case, they had expected it would happen eventually. But the expectation and the actual occurrence of it were two different things, something Bruce had never witnessed before. Or if he had, it hadn't sunk into his being the way watching his new friend crumble to the floor had done.

Now he felt completely helpless watching Harry struggle to return to consciousness. He was alive, but barely. Probably trying to decide if it was worth the effort to live after the way Marsha had run away, not caring at all what it did to her father. Yes, Bruce understood intellectually why she did what she did, but that didn't change the fact that she should have known better. No matter what this man did or didn't do, no one deserved to be treated that way.

Bruce wondered if he had met Harry when he was healthy, if they would have still become friends. He thought not. Harry would have probably been too busy to be a friend to anyone. And being too busy was one reason Harry was lying here without his daughter by his side.

Harry hadn't been too busy to observe his daughter, but he was too busy to meet her and get to know her. And Bruce knew Harry had remained too reserved and private to share his secret. Until now, when his time was running out.

Bruce could see why Marsha was angry and hurt. But running away would solve nothing. Bruce shook his head, wishing he had a magic wand and could send them both back in time to fix this before it was too late. Sighing, he leaned back in his chair and listened to the rhythmic beeps of the machines that were keeping his friend alive.

A few minutes later, Amir arrived with coffee and stood in the doorway, looking at the two men. Bruce had fallen asleep, his head resting on the hard edge of the chair, his long legs splayed out in front of him. Softly snoring.

Harry looked the same as before. So thin under the covers, it was as if he was barely there. Not that Harry had ever been a big man, always leaning to the thin side. But Harry's leanness had worked in his favor in the past. There would be times Amir would see Harry emerging from a meeting, his face and eyes so focused he looked like a bird of prey. Which, of course, is how he got the name Harry the Hawk.

Now Harry was a shriveled up version of himself. Amir knew Harry had to be hating the state that he was in, and that he was probably making a choice whether to let himself leave this world or stay. Amir thought Harry would hang on with his last breath to make things right with Marsha.

For years, he had watched over Marsha with Harry. Sometimes he would remain in the car waiting while Harry watched. Other times Harry would bring him in with him and they would sit together in the back of the auditorium watching Marsha sing and dance.

No matter what Marsha did, Harry would beam with happiness. Afterward, he'd always lean over to Amir and say, "Wasn't she wonderful?" And, of course, Amir would always agree that she was. And she was. But for Harry, Marsha was extraordinary.

Amir thought he was the epitome of a doting father, except it was all one sided. He hovered around the edges of Marsha's life, and Marsha never had the slightest idea that he was her biggest fan. She didn't know that when she left New York, Harry had mourned for her, knowing how much it hurt to give it up.

When Marsha moved back to Spring Falls, Harry had worried that she wouldn't be happy. He worried she was giving up dance and the theatre. And then when Marsha stayed in bed all morning, and rarely ventured out, Harry had fretted and worried even more.

When Ron bought April the house and she had asked Marsha to help her, and then do something arty with the downstairs, Harry had breathed a sigh of relief. Marsha was coming back.

And then Ron had ruined it all. Harry had confided in Amir that he felt as if it was his fault that Ron had gotten away with everything all those years because he hadn't taken the time to look Ron's way. If he had, he would have seen what was going on and stopped it.

That realization—that he missed the whole thing, and his daughter and her friends were affected by it—had robbed Harry of even more of his strength. Since then, Amir had watched Harry waste away more each day.

The doctors said it was because of AIDs, that nothing worked well anymore. But Amir knew Harry's feeling of guilt at not noticing the problem with Ron compounded it.

Watching Bruce and Harry sleep, Amir wondered if there was a land where people met when their bodies slept or died. Were Harry and Bruce talking to each other now? Were there other people there? Were there people that Harry could see waiting for him to cross to the other side?

Was there such a thing? Amir wondered. He hoped so. He hoped when it was his time that Harry would be there and they could talk together as equals and friends. Would they remember their time on this earth, or would they have to start again, only the essence of their being remembering who they once were?

Although he couldn't prove it, Amir believed that life kept going. That it came and stopped on a whim made little sense to him. But then, hardly anything did, really.

Which brought him back to the present. Why couldn't Harry find healing? Why couldn't his daughter give him what he wanted most, a moment where he was the father and she was his daughter? Just one moment is all Harry wanted. It wasn't asking much.

Bruce stirred, and Amir patted the inside of his jacket pocket where he kept what Harry had given him. Not for him to keep, but to give away when the time was right.

Amir was trying to stay out of wanting it to be now or later. All he really wanted was for his friend to be at peace, and then he would go home to his patient wife, and spend the rest of his days with her, and thank Harry for the time they got to spend together. To the world, he was just Harry's chauffeur, but to the two of them it had always been much more than that.

Thirty Four

J udith had finally learned that it was more effective to use the conference room when the Ruby Sisters had a meeting instead of trying to get everyone into her office. It used to work well when there were just the five of them, but their core group had expanded, and they had outgrown the chairs around her desk arrangement.

On the way to her office, she had called Booker and asked him to meet them there instead of the hospital. He was wise enough not to ask why. If Judith said come to the office, there was something up, and there was no point in trying to figure out what it was. And although Judith didn't call meetings unless it was important, she sounded upset. Judith's kind of upset. More intense than normal.

Judith had thought of asking Mary to come too, but decided that there was no need. At least not at this point. And she would have had Mimi and Janet come along with Nicky, but again, it didn't affect them directly, so there wasn't an urgent need. Besides, it would mean closing the gallery and then the whole town would start wondering what was up.

And since Judith didn't have anything she could prove yet, she didn't want to cause a stir over something that might be nothing, although she was fairly sure they had two problems. One, of course, was Marsha and her dad. And she couldn't even say for sure if April's friend was a problem or not.

But instead of pretending nothing was going on, she was going to bring it out into the open. She thought they could all agree they needed more facts about Ginny. Who was she? Where had she come from? Why was she in Spring Falls? And Judith would not discount Nicky's feeling of something being wrong. Was it as simple as Ginny just wanting to be April's friend, or was it something else?

All Judith knew for sure was they would not wait until something terrible happened before talking about it. They had all agreed. No secrets. Secrets were dangerous when they affected other people.

Judith didn't fool herself. She knew they all had secrets. She had a few. But she couldn't see how they affected anyone but herself. If that changed, she'd share them. But not until and if that ever happened.

Right now, Judith knew the problem with just feeling something was wrong was not enough to do anything with. It was much too amorphous, and she wanted more information. Something concrete they could focus on. She was hoping as a group they could pinpoint the problem.

Judith could have pretended to herself that she wasn't enjoying all this mystery, but she was. However, she didn't enjoy seeing her friends in pain, which meant she felt a hint of guilt at being happy that something different was happening in town again.

For years Spring Falls had been just a little too quiet. However, since Paul's death and the return of all the Ruby Sisters, things had changed. Judith hoped things could calm down for her friends, but that perhaps a mystery or two would pop up every once in a while. One that didn't involve her friends.

When Judith got a text from Bruce saying that Harry was in a coma and no one knew when or if he would come out of it, she asked him to come to the office too, and pulled up another chair to the table.

Nicky was the first to arrive, and Judith's heart leaped for joy when she saw how much better she looked than the first time she had seen her. Then, Nicky was hiding from the world, head down, mousy hair, dull eyes, sullen and afraid.

This time, if Judith hadn't been expecting Nicky, she wouldn't have known who it was. They stood and looked at each other for a second, both of them thinking of what it took for Nicky to be there, and then Judith asked, "You're not going to faint on me this time are you?"

Nicky laughed. "No, not this time."

Then there was a flurry of activity as Cindy, April, Marsha, and Bree came through the door. It took them all a moment to recognize Nicky before they exchanged hugs.

Only Marsha and April stood a little apart. Marsha felt surrounded by cotton padding and nothing but a dull roar was coming through. She barely registered that Nicky was there and being fussed over.

If Marsha didn't have Cindy guiding her to a chair, she probably would have just stood in the corner as if she was just a big stuffed animal. Not alive anymore.

She had the vague thought that no one understood what she was going through. But then, how could they? It had been her life, not theirs. They didn't know because she never told them.

Harry's revelation had hit her like a ton of bricks and now she was padded with cotton so she couldn't hear anything. She thought she liked it that way.

April, on the other hand, had stood back because she felt as if she was standing on the edge of a razor. Again. Everything was crystal clear. Noises, lights, too harsh and loud. Something was wrong. And it had to do with her. And she had just gotten on her feet again.

She had no reason to believe any of this, but the last time Nicky came to town, Nicky had blown up April's life. Was she going to do it again? April was pretty sure that was exactly what she was going to do. Not because she wanted to, but because it had to be done. But what was it this time?

Like Marsha, she wanted to run.

There was another interruption when Booker arrived, delighted to see Nicky back in Spring Falls. He and Nicky had spent some time together as they uncovered Ron's activities, and Booker felt protective towards her and Sara.

Over the last few months, Booker had gone to Jakestown a few times to check on the two of them. He claimed it was just to eat the famous hamburgers at the diner, but Nicky and Sara both knew it was more than that and were grateful. Nicky thought of him as the big brother they never had.

Booker hugged Nicky and then moved to sit next to Bree. Nicky saw Bree and Booker glance at each other and smiled to herself. Happy for them both. Booker had told her he and Bree were now just good friends, but watching their subtle interaction, she thought, *Sure, just friends.*

Then Bruce arrived and there was another moment when he paused and looked to make sure it was Nicky before exclaiming on how good she looked and hugging her too before sitting next to Judith. Nicky thought that no matter what happened on this visit, her inner self was much better off for coming.

"I ordered pizzas," Judith said. "Well, Nancy did. But let's put on the table the reasons for this meeting. And then we can eat and talk about them."

"Not talking," Marsha mumbled, knowing full well what one item on the agenda was.

"Well, you can remain silent, Marsha, but we will discuss the subject."

Booker, who didn't know what the meeting was about, just watched. He'd let Judith run the meeting. She was good at it. When it was over, Booker knew she would fill him in. But that Judith had asked him to come to the office meant that Judith thought something bad was happening, and it probably had to do with why Nicky was in town.

Bruce tried not to glare at Marsha, but he did anyway. She was running as she always did while Harry was fighting to stay alive just so he could spend a few precious moments with her. *Not fair,* Bruce thought.

"And then we have to discuss another very personal thing."

Judith paused for a moment, and then looked at April and April turned white.

Oh no, not again, she thought.

Cindy, sitting between Marsha and April, now turned her attention to April, ready to help as needed.

"It's that woman, Ginny," Judith said. "Who exactly is she, and what exactly is she doing here?"

Thirty Five

Ginny didn't get anywhere with her plan to find Mary and get to know her. Learning more about Mary wasn't part of Ginny's assignment. Which she found interesting, given that Mary was such an integral part of the story.

So she was pursuing the Mary angle to satisfy her own curiosity. *Besides*, Ginny thought, she might get information that she could use to free herself from the situation she was in. *That's a dangerous game you're playing, girl,* she said to herself and found she didn't care. It could be worth it.

But Mary hadn't been working and, cruising by her house, Ginny saw that both Mary and her husband Seth were home. Which meant there would be no getting to know her or breaking into Mary's house today.

Ginny was worried. So far she had nothing on anybody and she was due to report in that night. She had to have something by then. Of course, she could make a bunch of stuff up. How would he know if she was telling the truth or not?

But that kind of thinking was going to get her in real trouble. Ginny knew she couldn't underestimate him. He seemed to know everything. Well, not everything. That was why she was here in this stupid little town trying to drag out information from people she wouldn't have given the time of day to before.

Ginny used to think the best day of her life was the day she had met him. It had been years before when straight out of college she got a job at his company. She had liked his tall, dark, good looks, and loved how focused he was on the details of running the business. He was a grownup. Not like the sniveling college boys she could lead around by the nose.

But he wasn't interested in her at all. She had tried everything she could to seduce him. Every trick she knew which had always worked before. She knew all the buttons to push with men and even women to make them like her. They had always responded, and she'd play with them for a time. Then she'd get bored and move on. Ginny had been sure this guy would be different. If she could snag him, he would never bore her.

But this time her prey had remained aloof and untouchable. Over time, she had become desperate. She needed to know more. Maybe she was missing the trigger that would get him to notice her. So whenever she could, she followed him.

And one day, she followed him out of town. And that's when she learned who he really was. Ginny knew herself well, so it didn't surprise her that the knowledge made her love him more. He was everything she wanted to be, but she was too much of a coward.

Ginny thought about bribing him not for the money, but for the time she could spend with him. But decided against it. Too dangerous. And finally she had given up and moved on. As far as she knew, he did not even notice her leaving. Why would he? He had never noticed her presence.

For her part, she tried to forget the thrill that had raced through her when she thought of him. She blocked him out of her thinking as best as she could.

For the last few years, she had been making a pittance of a living as a free-lance journalist. She had dreams of writing the great American novel, but even the greatest fool in the world knew that was almost an impossibility. And Ginny was not a fool.

So, like her dream of becoming someone special to the man she admired and wanted, she put that dream aside and wrote stupid little stories for small town newspapers. Doing what she was doing wasn't enough to live on, so she used men to pay her bills, giving them what they wanted, but getting very little pleasure from the transaction.

Then one day her cell phone rang, but Ginny hadn't recognized the number, so she didn't answer. They called again, and she still didn't answer. And then she got a text that said, "Answer!"

Now Ginny wished with all her heart she had never answered. She should have destroyed her phone, packed up and moved far away. Changed her name. All of that would have been better than answering that call.

But she did none of those things. Instead, the next time it rang, she answered and everything changed.

If only I said no and he had let that be okay, she sometimes thought. *Sure, if only pigs could fly. Nothing was going to change the fact that she answered the phone and said yes to the request.*

Now Ginny knew it hadn't been a request. It had been an order. However, at the time, her heart had skipped a beat when she heard his voice and she would have said yes to anything he asked.

Which was ridiculous because he didn't say his name and she didn't ask him to either. She knew who it was. He knew she knew who he was. And they both knew what he was capable of. Still, Ginny had felt special and needed and happy that out of all the people he could have called, he called her.

"Listen," he said. "Do you want to make some money writing a story for me?"

At that point, Ginny would have said yes if he had told her to jump off the Brooklyn Bridge to see if she could fly. As long as he would be there to catch her, she would do it.

And that's what he promised. He'd be there for her. Just write the story. "After that, it's you and me," he had said.

And like every stupid woman she had ever despised for their willingness to do something for some lame-brained, stupid man, she had said yes.

Not to a lame-brained stupid man, but to a brilliant and dangerous one. What had made it even worse is she knew who he was, and she hadn't cared. He promised they'd be together. All she had to do was get some information and write a story. How hard could that be?

Well, it was turning out to be extremely hard. These women were impossible. And April, who looked like such an easy target, had hardened against her since they had come to Spring Falls.

All the doors were closed to her. But he had given her a deadline and her time was running out. Ginny knew it wouldn't be a simple firing if she failed. Despite loving him with a passion, she knew he was using her, and she was only as useful as the information he wanted. If she couldn't provide it, she was disposable. He would get rid of her one way or another.

Ginny had another option, one she hoped she didn't have to use. But she would if she needed to. It wasn't exactly what she wanted. She wanted him. So she needed to give him what he wanted and hope that bought her a little time in his world.

Thirty Six

After asking all those questions about Ginny, the group realized they knew nothing at all about her. It didn't matter that they all agreed that she was up to something. But what?

Of course, they suspected it had to do with Ron. After all, she befriended April for a reason. What else could it be?

"And here I thought she liked me just because I'm me," April said, trying to make light of the situation, but feeling once again that she was stupid and useless.

Cindy reached out and squeezed April's arm, leaning over and whispering, "Well, we do!"

"Here's what I don't get," Bree said, paying no attention to April's distress. "Why is she acting so blatantly abrasive? She must know that any reasonable person would shut down around someone like that. Why not be sweet and charming? Friendly? As she must have been when you first met her, April.

"What changed when she came to Spring Falls? Is she behaving this way so we suspect her of subterfuge? But for what end?"

"Maybe she doesn't know she changed?" Bruce suggested.

Judith shook her head. "No, she's too smart for that. She wants information from us, and yet is acting in such a way that no one will give it to her. What is the game she is playing? Does she want us to suspect her?"

"So what do I do?" April said.

"How do you feel about giving her what she wants?" Booker asked.

"What do you mean?"

"When she asks a question, give her a straight answer. Just enough to keep her from asking more questions. Maybe call her out on her inappropriate behavior. If you just ignore it, she'll know something is wrong. It's what you would do with each other, isn't it?"

Bruce stole a glance at Marsha. She was sitting beside Cindy, looking distant and mad at the same time. Booker was right. They should not be ignoring Marsha's behavior, either. But it couldn't be him that spoke to her. He was too mad at her.

"Okay," April sighed. "I'll talk to her as if she is my daughter. Call her out, and have a heart to heart with her. But she had me fooled while we were on the road. It was only when we got here that I began to suspect she was playing me all along. But again, why? If it's Ron, what does he want?"

"I think we can all agree. He wants you, April," Bree said. "The question is, how does having this woman in town asking questions serve that purpose?"

Judith stepped in. "Well, now that we have all agreed that Ginny is up to something, let's find out some answers. I have my sources. Booker has his. We'll get to work and let you all know what we learn. And April, please don't go anywhere alone. You're safe in the house—even though she is there. But get one of us to go with you when you leave."

"Well, now you are scaring me again."

Judith just looked at April, and everyone knew that was her intention. Better to be afraid and prepared, than happy and in danger.

Looking around the room, she added, "Actually, maybe no one should go anywhere alone until we find out what is happening. Maybe there is no danger. Maybe it's not Ron. But if it is Ron, he could use one of us to get to April."

Nicky sat through the discussion, saying nothing. Something had brought her to Spring Falls. Now she knew it was probably something to do with Ron, and it made a little more sense. What she needed to do was meet this Ginny and find out what she wanted.

Nancy knocked on the conference room door, but no one needed to ask what she wanted. The smell of pizza had already drifted into the office. So they took a break. As they ate, they chatted about the weather, what they had seen on Instagram or TikTok.

Judith thought of it as a mental palate cleanser.

Once the last piece of pizza was gone, she said it was time to talk about Harry, reviewing the situation for Booker's benefit.

"Is that Harry the Hawk Harrison? The man behind the success of multiple companies? That Harry? And he is Marsha's long-lost, but not really lost, father? Wow! That's a story I'd love to hear more about," Booker said, glancing at the still sullen Marsha.

"Yes, that Harry, and yes, Marsha's not so lost father."

"So, since he is lying in a coma in the hospital right now, what do you think about getting Bryan and Rachel to come back and help him? Bryan helped me come back to the living. Maybe he can help Harry?" April asked.

"That's a good idea," Bree answered. "It can't hurt, anyway. We all witnessed how it worked, even if we don't understand how. They can stay at my place."

"Yes," Bruce said, thinking at this point, anything would be useful. "How soon can they get here? I'm not sure how much time Harry has left, if any, really."

Bruce glared at Marsha, who simply turned away, only hearing his words as if they were far off and muffled. If anything, the cotton padding around her was getting thicker. Marsha wondered if that meant she was leaving too, just like Harry. But she was still sitting up in Judith's conference room, so she must still be alive.

Bree took out her phone and texted Bryan. While they waited for an answer, they planned what to do to next.

Judith asked Cindy to take Marsha to her house. If she could, she would stop by later. Cindy knew what that meant. They were going to work together to reach Marsha. Hopefully, they wouldn't make her mood worse.

Cindy agreed with Bruce's glaring at Marsha. Sure, it was disturbing to hear that your father was alive after all this time, but it was no reason to retreat into that stony silence. She had enough of Marsha's moods.

Bree asked Nicky if she would come to the woods to get Marsha's car.

"Good idea," Cindy said. "And then Nicky, come stay with me and Marsha. You can bring your car to my house now, and Bree can pick you up and take you to the woods. Then you could bring Marsha's car to my house and stay with me while you are in town."

Nicky nodded yes, smiling at Cindy. She was looking forward to getting to know her better.

"Booker, could you and Bruce stay for a minute?" Judith asked. They both nodded yes.

Bree's phone beeped. She read the message and texted back.

"Bryan said okay. They'll be here tomorrow morning."

Bruce said thanks, hoping that they would be in time to help Harry, while Cindy hoped that would give them enough time to get Marsha to return to the land of the living so she could be there for Harry if he woke up.

As Bree stood to leave, she and Booker exchanged looks. Once again, Nicky noticed and wondered if she could get more information from Bree on the ride to the woods.

Or perhaps Bree doesn't realize what's happening? Nicky wondered. *Doubtful. Bree is too self-aware. But maybe she is pretending it isn't happening.*

Watching everyone prepare to go their separate ways, but with the same purpose in mind, Nicky was glad she came to Spring Falls. She could take part in the uncovering of this mystery woman, Ginny, watch a budding romance unfold, and be part of a father and daughter reunion.

It could be wonderful. If everything goes well, Nicky thought.

Seeing the sullen Marsha, feeling April's fear, and looking at Bruce's worried face, she wasn't so sure it would.

Thirty Seven

"Are you up for a trip?" Bryan Anderson asked.

He and his wife Rachel had just returned from having lunch at the Diner and were sitting outside on a park bench that faced the woods, sipping cups of coffee, watching the birds flit from tree to tree, when he got the text from Bree.

Everywhere Bryan looked, something was popping out of the ground. Flowers of all colors were bobbing in the breeze. The forsythia's yellow stems framed the gate that led out to the path into the woods that ran for miles behind their house, the yellow glow making it look like a portal into another world. In some ways, it was. Things happened in the woods that happened nowhere else. He spent as much time as possible in that other world. Besides being with Rachel, it was his favorite place to be.

Spring was a time of awakening for everything—including people in the in-between. Which meant for Bryan it was a very busy time of year. More people in the in-between decided that it was time to move on in the spring, and came to him for help. Maybe they woke up like nature did after a rest.

Bryan wondered if spring was like that on the other side of the world. Maybe they could take a trip down-under sometime. But for this trip, they would not be going far.

He was up for it, if only to have a change of scenery, but also because he had enjoyed the town of Spring Falls. In many ways, it was like their town of Doveland. Small, friendly, set aside from the rest of the world.

Of course, Spring Falls had a small community college, and they didn't, which meant there were more young people strolling the streets. More coffee shops. More diverse restaurants. Which added to the pleasure of making the trip.

"Sure," Rachel said, thinking that it was her busiest time of the year but that she could use a few days away, anyway. People started looking for houses in the spring. *Just like birds*, she thought.

But Doveland was a small town, and there were never that many buyers and sellers. No one wanted the town to get any bigger, and many of the town hall meetings had been about how to prevent the urban sprawl that blighted so much of the country.

One suggestion was to create a green belt circle around the town. The land would be owned by a trust and would manage the land and leave it undeveloped. They had heard of other towns which were doing that and thought it might work in Doveland. The town council had asked Rachel to lead the committee that would begin the research on how to accomplish it. She knew it would be a lot of work, but it would be worth it if they could pull it off. She thought she could.

"Sure. Where to?"

"Spring Falls."

Rachel's face lit up, her green eyes sparkling with happiness. Looking at her, Bryan marveled once again how beautiful she was and how lucky he was that Rachel loved him. And over the past year, their longtime attachment to each other had only deepened.

Bryan had begun to understand, rather late in life, he thought, that love was not the romanticized version sold in books and songs, but the steady commitment of a shared life, and the desire to support each other in all ways. Rachel's beauty amazed him, but it was her compassion, her strength, and obvious joy at being with him, that made him treasure her.

Plus, Bryan knew without her he would fold under the pressure of being in almost constant demand for his services. He didn't get phone calls or emails. He got people popping up everywhere. And not all of them were good people.

Only recently had he learned how to shut the door—so to speak—to everyone, and then only admit those people he was willing to have in his mental space. Even though most of them moved on quickly, there was always a residual energy left that he had to remove from around him. Otherwise, Bryan felt as if he was being encased in a layer of dirt. Not real dirt. Energy dirt.

Rachel had helped him with that, too. He counted on her seeing through the pretense of people, and in that way, she was protective of him. Rachel said it wasn't just her protecting him. She was protecting herself, too. She had waited years for him to get the courage to approach her and she wasn't about to lose him now.

His job was to not put too much stress on her. Because as perfect as she was, if she wanted to, she could shut down emotionally, stop talking, or just say no to everything for a while until she got her balance back.

Although in times like that, Bryan understood why it happened, he didn't like it when it did. So he always asked her before making plans if it was something she wanted. And he had become more attentive, trying to anticipate what would please her.

Rachel clapped her hands together in excitement and her ponytail bobbed up and down, flashing a streak of red into the air.

She really liked the people she met in Spring Falls and was looking forward to seeing them again.

Then she stopped in horror. "Wait. Why are we going? Is something wrong with one of the Ruby Sisters?"

"No. It appears there is a friend of theirs that needs help. Bree said it was not someone we know."

"Did she say who it was?"

"No. Just that it was an emergency and wondered if we could come right away."

Rachel looked out over the woods behind their house, the trees so green she felt as if she could breathe in the color, and thought how lucky she was. She could go on an adventure with the man she adored and do good at the same time. How wonderful was that? Plus, maybe get to know the people they met there just a little better. And help someone. Really, what could be better than that?

"Yes," she said again.

As Bryan texted back that they would be there in the morning, Rachel waited to see how she felt about whomever they were going to help. Sometimes it worked. She'd get a sense of a person and would let Bryan know so he could be prepared.

This time, she felt two things. One was compassion and sorrow, and the other was fear. Was this all about the same person? Or was there something else going on in Spring Falls?

Taking Bryan's hand, she told him what she felt. He nodded. He had felt that fear, too. But who was it for? Were they walking into a problem?

"Are you sure we should go?" he asked Rachel.

"Yes. But we need to be careful," she answered, and wondered if they should let Bree know. And then realized that Bree already knew.

Thirty Eight

For Nicky, the ride out to the woods with Bree was surreal. The last time she had been in Spring Falls, she and Bree had barely spoken. Now she knew it was because Bree was hiding the secret that her daughter Mary had resulted from Ron raping her. A secret she had successfully hidden until Nicky came to town and exposed Ron.

Nicky had worried that Bree might never forgive her for it. Instead, Bree had thanked her for setting her free, and for her bravery. And now they were traveling in a car together like old friends.

Bree asked her how she and Sara were doing, and Nicky told her they were doing well. They still had bad days, but they were grateful to be reunited after all these years.

"Sara has trouble forgiving herself for hiding all these years. She blames herself for our parents dying since they gave up after she left. She knows the town essentially shut down because they suspected each other. All the joy the people of Jakestown had died when she disappeared. Given all that, I keep telling her how brave she is to return and face what happened after she left.

"And of course she deals with the guilt of wondering if she would have told what happened to her instead of running, how many lives might have been saved. But would anyone have believed her then? It was possible they wouldn't have. It was a different time then. Not sure it's much better now."

Bree nodded, thinking how she had told no one either. She understood the guilt that Sara carried. She carried it too.

"Booker told me he enjoys visiting and watching the town recover. He says he goes for the burgers, but I know he is checking up on the two of you."

"And we appreciate that. Even though we pretend he's only there for Sara's food. I think he feels guilty for not catching Ron yet, and he worries Ron will seek revenge. He made us get a security system for the house and the restaurant, even though we don't own either."

"I know what you mean. I agree. He does feel guilty. And afraid for us too. He made us all get security systems. We don't talk about it much. But I can feel his worry. But really, why would Ron come back?"

Nicky thought about all that she knew about Ron and knew that if he didn't get what he wanted, he would want revenge. But would he choose revenge over freedom? He must know that coming back would put him in danger of being caught.

"Well, we know Ron needs to feel as if he is the smartest person in the room. And he wants to always be the one in control. We are the ones that took that control away from him, and in his mind, I am sure Ron believes we are responsible for him losing April.

"So, yes, I think he might decide to do something to punish us, and maybe to get April back. He's a planner. He thinks things through and figures out how to accomplish what he wants. Besides, we know he loves the hunt. And we know he loves April. Combine how hurt he feels with the need to control and it definitely means he could choose vengeance over freedom. Especially if he believes he could get away with it and have both."

By then Bree had reached the trail's parking lot and had pulled in beside Marsha's car. Turning to look at Nicky, she asked, "Are you afraid?"

"Honestly, I am always afraid. I'm afraid of losing Sara again. Not just because of Ron, but because she carries all that guilt. I'm afraid I'll never find anyone to love, because who would love me? And yes, I am afraid of Ron. Not just for me, but for everyone he knows. And I'm afraid I'll give up and retreat inside myself again. I got really good at living that way after Sara disappeared.

"And I live in fear that the people I have come to care about, in Jakestown, and here in Spring Falls, will give up on me. Or even worse, be angry and upset with what I have done."

Nicky flopped back in her seat, spent, afraid that she had let out all those words, especially to Bree, who always seemed so in control of herself. She waited for Bree's reaction. She expected her to be both angry and disappointed in her. Why wouldn't Bree be that and so much more?

A soft breeze drifted through the window Bree had opened, and Bree heard the crows again calling to each other and wondered if birds and animals ever had a thought of vengeance or guilt.

"I'm sorry," Bree said, hoping Nicky would feel the depth of what she meant by those words.

Nicky turned to look at Bree, her eyes glittering with tears, and said, "Thank you."

Neither of them needed to say more. They knew what they each meant.

Nicky reached over and hugged Bree, and taking Marsha's keys, stepped out of the car. Turning, and leaning in, she said, "Thank you," one more time.

Bree smiled, and made a heart with her hands, thinking that sometimes even writers didn't know the right words to say.

As Nicky drove away, they waved at each other, and then Bree sat back in her seat and thought about her life, and what Nicky had said about Ron and his desire for vengeance. But most of all, she worried about the fact that Ron must now know he had another child. Would he care? And if he did, what would he do about it?

Perhaps it was time to talk to April about the fact that their children were half-siblings, and ask Booker to add security for Mary, Seth, and Rho.

Looking at the woods in front of her, Bree decided she needed a walk in the woods. Closing the window, she turned off the car, grabbed a hat, sunglasses, keys, and phone, and stepped out into a glorious spring day.

Yes, she had been here already today, but how could it hurt to walk twice in one day? Glancing up at the crows sitting in the trees at the edge of the woods, facing the parking lot, she thought they looked like guards watching over their territory.

Looking up at them, Bree smiled and said, "Thank you for watching over us today."

She could have sworn they nodded to her. And then they took off down the path in front of her. She followed, grateful that at least for the moment, she felt safe.

Thirty Nine

Nicky arrived at Cindy's to find both of them sitting in the living room waiting for her. Cindy was sitting on the couch, her legs folded up under her, sipping a cup of coffee, looking frustrated.

Marsha was slumped in a chair turned as far away from facing Cindy as was possible. She didn't look up when Nicky came in the door.

"Grab a drink, Nicky, and join us," Cindy said, patting the couch.

Nicky took a can of soda from the refrigerator and settled in beside Cindy. Marsha still hadn't looked at either of them.

When Cindy shrugged, mouthing, "I can't get through," Nicky leaned forward to speak to Marsha.

"I think I know how you feel. I know it's not the same thing as what happened between you and your father, but it's close.

"Even though I went looking for Sara, I did it because I didn't know what else to do. I thought she was dead. And although I loved her, I was furious with her. In a way, I guess, I still am.

Especially now that I know she was hiding the whole time while the rest of us suffered.

"I know what happened to her wasn't her fault. But what she did afterwards was devastating to everyone. I feel as if I have wasted my entire life because of her decision.

"I had dreams before she left. I thought I would be somebody. What that person was, I didn't know. But I believed I could choose any life for myself. And then it all disappeared.

"Sure. I could have left it alone. I tried. But that only made it worse. Then I started obsessing about finding out what happened. And while I did that, I turned myself into a nobody, so I would never have to interact with anyone again meaningfully.

"I loved my sister, my parents, and even though I complained about Jakestown while I lived there, I loved it for what it had given me. And then all of that was ripped away in just a moment of time."

Nicky took a sip of soda before continuing, taking a beat to see if Marsha was responding. She couldn't tell.

"Even now, I wake up terrified that this new life is a dream. That the nightmare I was living was reality. Each morning, I have to choose again to live my life forward, not backward.

"I have Sara back. Maybe not the kid sister she once was, but it's still Sara. I have a family. And for years I didn't. So yes, I understand how it must feel to find a family that you must have thought you lost years ago.

"Maybe you feel betrayed, angry at him for leaving you, for making what to you feels like a mean and selfish choice. Just like I feel sometimes when I think of Sara.

"But at the time, they didn't do what they did to us on purpose. Sara ran because she was afraid and ashamed. I don't know your father, but I think he must have felt the same way. Sara thought she was doing the right thing. She didn't mean to hurt us all the way she did.

"Your father didn't mean to hurt you. He obviously never stopped loving you. Perhaps for the wrong reason, he made the choice to stay away. But it was never intended to hurt you.

"And your mom. I suppose you could be angry at her for what she did. Making him stay away. But she, too, thought she was doing the right thing.

"You and I, Marsha, have to forgive these people for hurting us. We can see how our lives could have been better if they hadn't made the choices they did. But now, it's our choice of what to do.

"I have chosen to love my sister with all her flaws, and despite the pain she caused me. For your own well-being, I think you need to make the same choice about your father. And unlike me, who hopefully has many years left to work out issues I have with Sara, while building a life with her, you have a few days, or hours, if that.

"You'll never be able to live with it if you don't forgive him for his stupid ass choice and get to know him, if only briefly."

As Nicky talked, Cindy watched in awe. She had never heard Nicky speak more than a few sentences at a time. And Nicky had never shared what it felt like to be abandoned.

When Nicky had started speaking, Marsha stared at the wall in front of her, her face both angry and distant. But as Nicky spoke, Cindy watched the anger disappear as Marsha closed her eyes, tears creeping down her cheeks. She didn't bother to wipe them away. Just sat motionless and listened.

Finally, Marsha turned and faced Cindy and Nicky, closed her eyes again, and took a deep breath before speaking.

"I hear you. All of what you said is true. I should be grateful that I had a father somewhere, and who has been watching over me. And I get to know him. Maybe. Or maybe I killed him by walking out the door.

"And you're right. I'll never forgive myself for that if he dies now without me speaking to him. And yes, I am angry. Angry at my mother for sending him away. Angry about the way he was treated, and angry at his choices.

"But it's more than that. It's who he is, and what he said."

When Marsha didn't go on, Nicky leaned forward and asked, "What do you mean, Marsha? Is it because he's gay? That's not his fault. That wasn't a choice. And besides, why would you care?"

Marsha shook her head. She'd been hiding her secret her entire life. Telling no one. Living with it inside herself. Trying to be what people thought she was. And then Harry brought it all out and made her face it. Harry, her father, was a gay man. And he hadn't hidden it. But it had changed both their lives in ways that could never be repaired.

It's now or never, Marsha thought. She felt her entire body vibrating in anticipation and wondered if it would shatter when she spoke.

"I'm gay," Marsha said, and then waited for the world to fall in on her. The world she had so carefully constructed so that no one would ever find out.

Cindy put her coffee on the table, leaned over to hold Marsha's hand as she said, "Oh, honey. We knew that already."

Forty

*W*ell, I didn't, Nicky thought. *But then I had so much on my mind last time I was in Spring Falls, I wouldn't have noticed if she had six fingers.* And compared to the trauma they had faced with Ron, this seemed trivial to her. But obviously not to Marsha.

That's what comes from keeping secrets, Nicky thought. *They go from being a small stone you might trip on in life to an enormous boulder blocking everything out.*

Marsha and Cindy were hugging, Marsha sobbing so hard Cindy had to bring her to the couch to sit with her. Nicky moved to the chair to let them have the space they needed.

Finally Marsha asked, "What do you mean you all know? Who all knows?"

"Well, all the Ruby Sisters know. Who else, I don't know. We never spoke about it to anyone."

Marsha sat up and pulled away from Cindy. "You all spoke about this? Like gossiping about me behind my back?"

"Of course not. You know us better than that. I think we talked about it once in high school, and we waited for you to tell us, or act on it. But you never did."

"In high school? You've known since I was in high school? How? What did I ever do to make you think that? I had boyfriends. Sorta."

As the realization hit Marsha that she had hidden a secret all her life that didn't need to be a secret, Marsha blurted out, "I have another secret."

Cindy and Nicky looked at each other, momentarily afraid.

"I was raped by Ron, too. At Bree's wedding. I am responsible too for what he went on to do."

A cloud went across the sun, temporarily darkening the room. Marsha felt it was a sign that she was right about herself. She was a failure and a disgrace. And the cotton padding that she had surrendered herself to before, and that had only just dissolved as she listened to Nicky, started forming around her again.

Then she looked at Cindy, who wasn't looking at her as if she was a monster, or with pity, but with a straight, clear-sighted love.

"Did you know this too?"

"I did," Cindy said.

"How? Why didn't you say?"

"I wanted to. It was such a burden for you to carry. But I heard by mistake as you were telling Janet and Mimi and I didn't want you to think you were being spied on."

Marsha looked at Nicky, expecting to see disgust or hate on her face, and seeing neither, the shell she had built around her started to dissolve. The cloud moved past the sun, and Cindy's living room filled with light.

For Marsha, it was a symbol of what was possible for her. She could feel light and be free again, the way she used to feel when she danced around the living room as a child.

All she had ever wanted then was to be a dancer. But not only did she love the feeling of dancing, she had secretly hoped her father would one day see her and love her. Because, despite pretending that it was okay, she had wanted her father. She wanted to know why he had abandoned her and her mother. But mostly, she wanted her father to love her and be proud of her. Wherever he was.

All her life, she had believed that her father hadn't wanted to know her. Which meant she wasn't good enough. And once she realized how different she was, she became afraid that if her friends found out who she was, and what had happened to her, they would abandon her. Just as her father had done.

But now, she knew it had all been a lie. She hadn't needed to hide herself from the world. She didn't need to have kept either secret.

It had all been her fault. It was her fault that she wasn't living that life she dreamed of as she danced around the living room. It had all been a lie that she had told herself. She was a coward and a failure.

"Oh, God," she gasped, standing, trying to keep herself from running out of the room the way she always did. She was shaking so hard her teeth started chattering.

It was Nicky who understood the avalanche of emotions that Marsha was feeling. She stood, grabbed her shoulders, and turned Marsha to face her.

And then, using the strongest voice she could, she gathered her strength and poured it into Marsha.

"Don't start blaming yourself, Marsha. If you do, you will be sucked under again. You will be of no use to anyone. Now is the time to claim your right to be yourself.

"I promise you, I know this battle you are fighting. And you must win. You must not let guilt and shame, or even anger, take over again. Your friends need you. Your father needs you.

"You've done the hard part. Now let it go. Remember who you are. Be proud of it. You are one of the luckiest people I know. You have talent and grace and beauty and friends. Everything else is a weed. Don't let it grow inside you anymore.

"Say no to it, Marsha. Please."

Marsha took a ragged breath and, tipping her head down to Nicky, asked, "Do you really think I can do this?"

"I have no doubt at all."

"Me either," Cindy said, joining the two of them.

Nicky knew what Marsha needed to do next. She took Marsha's car keys out of her pocket and put them into Marsha's hand. She took a tissue and dabbed Marsha's tears away, bringing back memories of doing the same for her sister when she had fallen down and skinned her knee.

"Now, go. We'll meet you there."

"Thank you," Marsha whispered to the two of them.

As she drove to the hospital Marsha continued to thank them, and to thank whatever god had brought her back to herself. She remembered now what she wanted, and April had given her a place to do it. The Ruby House. Now all she had to do was go make peace with her father.

"Please," she whispered to whatever god was listening, "Please don't let me be too late."

Marsha wondered briefly if it was the same god who had made her into a freak that she was praying to, and then remembered that wasn't true. That was the lie part. The weed that Nicky had told her to pull out.

I'm good just the way I am and I am going to prove it, Marsha said to herself. *And dang it, dad, stay alive long enough for me to tell you that.* And then Marsha realized she had called Harry, "dad," and smiled to herself.

Yes, she was going to remember everything about her dreams and do them. And her dad was going to be proud of her. But first she was going to be proud of herself.

All she had to do now was make it to the hospital in time.

Forty One

After everyone left, Judith, Bruce, and Booker stayed in the conference room for a few more minutes. Judith asked Booker if he would look into Ginny's background. Was she really who she said she was? Booker agreed, making phone calls on his way out the door.

Judith and Bruce moved to her office, shut the door, and sat on the couch together.

"I'm sorry about Harry," Judith said.

Bruce only nodded. What could he say? He was sorry too. Because no matter what happened with Marsha and Harry, he was still going to lose a friend. The best he could hope for was that Harry would gain a little peace before leaving.

"Are you giving up, Bruce?" Judith asked. "I mean, he could recover and live longer than you thought. He's a fighter. Fight for him to stay. Maybe long enough that you could teach him how to play chess. That is, if he doesn't already know and could beat the pants off of you."

Bruce laughed, stood, and pulled Judith up to hug her. He loved the way she felt in his arms. They fit together perfectly.

"You're right." Kissing her on the forehead, he said, "I'll be at the hospital if you need me."

Driving home, Judith decided. She would do what she had told Bruce to do. Fight for her friend.

Walking in her front door, Judith thought the house felt like a freezer even though she had cranked up the heat before leaving that morning. Spring could be cold sometimes. But with Ginny in the house, it felt like an iceberg.

Since she didn't see Ginny or April in the living room or kitchen, she assumed they were both in their rooms, so she called out to them to come to the kitchen.

It took a moment before they both came downstairs and shuffled into the kitchen. Neither of them looked pleased to be there. But Judith didn't care. She gestured for them to sit at the kitchen table.

"Coffee? Soda?"

When neither of them said anything, Judith waited a beat and then sat down and looked at them both, and thought how much she loved what she was going to do. Get answers. Fix it.

Smiling, the tips of her red hair lighting up for a moment, she said, "Let's talk."

April trembled a little and dropped her head to stare at the table. Ginny lifted her head and glared at Judith, the pupils in her brown eyes flaring.

Oh good, Judith thought. *She wants to play it that way. It makes it easier for me. I don't have to pretend to be nice.* It was time to get some straight answers.

Marsha found both Bruce and Amir sitting by her father's bed. One on each side. Amir looked as if he was sleeping, but as soon as she walked into the room, he stood up.

Bruce turned and smiled, his heart lifting a little. Marsha looked different. Her face had softened, and her eyes were red. The stony mask was gone.

"May I stay with you?" Marsha asked the two men.

"Amir and I were just going to get something to drink," Bruce said, walking out the door. Amir was right behind him, giving Marsha's hand a squeeze of reassurance as he passed her.

Marsha watched them go and then sat down in the chair where Bruce had been and stared at the man in the bed. Did she see any of herself in him? Yes, they were both tall. *So that must be from him*, she thought.

And although his eyes were closed, she had seen them as he had stared at her with hope at Cindy's house. Harry's eyes were almost hidden under heavily drooping eyelids, but she had seen enough to know they were gray like hers.

Were those two things enough to make her feel connected to him? She didn't think so. Besides, she still wasn't sure she wanted to feel connected.

A crust of resentment was still in place around her heart. She closed her eyes, not looking at the form in the bed, but trying to feel what it would be like if she had known this man all her life and cared about him.

Without thinking about it, Marsha found herself talking to the man in the bed as if he could hear her. She told him what had just happened at Cindy's house. She asked him if he had been there when her dance partner had dropped her as he was lifting her. Did he see it? Did he worry if she would ever dance again? Had he come to the hospital and watched over her?

Did he see himself in her? Did he worry about how she was dealing with it in the world? Did he know what Ron had done? Did he do anything about it?

"I could have used you by my side, Harry." she said. "I needed a father that I could reach out and touch, not a stranger who knew me from afar. It wasn't fair," she told him. "This isn't fair. Not at all."

And finally she asked him to stay, if only for a little while, so she could talk about all the things she had wanted to confide in a father all her life. And never did. The little things, and the big thing that had tied her up in knots. She wanted to know how he had dealt with being different. Did he learn how? Could she?

"Stay and be a real father, please," she begged, astonishing herself with her need for his affection.

When Bruce and Amir returned an hour later, they found her sound asleep, her head resting on the side of the bed, Harry's hand in hers. Silently they pulled up another chair for Bruce, and settled in, waiting for whatever was coming next. Whatever it would be, they would be there to witness it.

And Bruce thought, *I'll be here to support Amir and Marsha, while Judith hunts down answers for the rest of the Ruby Sisters.* He smiled to himself and closed his eyes, thinking how much he loved Judith.

Later, when Cindy and Nicky peeked into Harry's room, they saw Marsha asleep holding her father's hand, and both Bruce and Amir with their eyes closed.

Seeing they weren't needed, they stepped out into the hall and Cindy said, "Let's go to Judith's."

Nicky agreed. She still needed to talk to April and see that Ginny person. Maybe she could figure out why she had felt such a sense of danger that it had brought her to Spring Falls. She was sure that Ginny was the reason. But why?

Forty Two

Ron Page was sure Ginny was failing at her job. But he expected her to. Ginny Lynn was a pathetic mouse of a woman. Of course, she thought she was special, strong, smart. Smarter than him. But she wasn't. No one was.

Because here he was in town, right under their noses, and not one person knew it. Ginny thought he was contacting her from far away, and her reward for doing what he asked would be that they would be together.

That Ginny could have ever thought that would happen confirmed to him she was a stupid, stupid woman. The only woman he ever wanted to be with was April.

And now April was only a few houses away. He could snatch her and run away with her any time he wanted to. But the last time he tried that, she had almost killed herself trying to get away from him.

No. Now it would be different. Now he would have to be absolutely sure that she would stay and that would take a little more planning.

Instead of a plea to come with him, it would be a threat. One she couldn't run away from. He knew his April. She would never put someone else in danger.

He was in no rush. At the moment he was thoroughly enjoying being a voyeur and outsmarting everyone around him. He had always treasured this part of the hunt.

Now he was applying his years of practice to the most important prey of all. His wife. Everyone thought he was the object of their hunt, and instead, they were the targets of his hunt.

It's a wonderful turn of events, Ron thought to himself as he stroked the mustache he had grown. His hair, too, was different. A different color, longer and pulled back into a ponytail. Sure, it wasn't his, but it looked like it was.

Ron was as far from looking like a successful businessman as he could get himself. At least as far as he was willing to go. Filth was disgusting. He couldn't go there.

He watched as Cindy and that bitch Nicky arrived at Judith's. Probably to talk about him. *How delicious,* Ron thought. *Three Ruby sisters in one place.* Plus, the one who outed him. It made his job easier. He didn't have to go to Jakestown to get her.

And because he had access to the trackers Ginny had put on all their cars, he knew Bree was in the woods, and Marsha was with her daddy at the hospital.

Sitting in his car sipping his coffee, Ron mused over that turn of events. Harry was an element he hadn't expected. How could he have? No one had known that Marsha had a very famous and very wealthy father. He wondered how he could use Harry's presence to make his plan even better.

He had set up this plan years before. It was a just-in-case plan. And Ginny had always been part of it, even though she didn't know that. Ginny had thought he hadn't noticed her when she arrived at his office all fresh-faced and eager. He had.

But he didn't believe in having affairs. It was wrong. And complexly unnecessary. Besides, he hated her crude attempts at getting him to fall for her. For a moment, he had entertained the thought of making her one of his conquests, but he had long ago decided not to mess around with women he knew. That was too dangerous.

He had made that mistake with Nicky's sister. But he was only fifteen. And she was his first, so what did he know? And then he tried out April's friends, Bree and Marsha, but that was a mistake, too. They could have told April. But they didn't. Leaving him free to practice his art and learn what to do and not to do.

Now he played away from anyone he knew. And he had become an expert at hiding in plain sight. He knew how to look different. To stand and walk differently. To change how he moved his hands. No one would recognize his body movements, no one would recognize his face. He was safe. And he was near.

He hoped Ginny was failing miserably, making every Ruby Sister suspect her motives. He wanted them to figure out that it was him that had sent her. That little sniveling useless woman. Once she succeeded in what he had sent her to do, he could get rid of her. He hated having partners of any kind. Except April, of course.

Ron took another sip of his coffee, the one he had purchased as a takeaway from Judith and Cindy's favorite coffee shop. They were right. It was delicious. He thought about having dinner at ParaTi's. He was hungry, and it would be so satisfying to be in the restaurant where their friend Mary worked.

Bree's daughter. Actually, his daughter. Of course, that was why Bree had left town all those years ago. He had produced a child. Confirming once again how stupid he had been when he first started this adventure. Now he was so much smarter and safer. But still. He had a daughter, and now a granddaughter, right here in Spring Falls.

Yes, he thought to himself. *And I have another daughter, and a son and grandson. But who cares? I don't need them to get April. Everything I need to have her be mine again is right here in front of me.*

Besides, his daughter and her husband had guards. He could get past them, but why bother? *And my cowardly son is running around Europe with his partner. A man. Disgusting.*

If he had time and it wasn't too much effort, he would punish Robert for acting that way. But there wasn't, and he wasn't worth the effort. Let him live his life in sin. Who cared? The only thing that made any difference to him was that Robert's behavior might reflect badly on him. How could he raise a pansy?

Probably April's fault, anyway. She came from that line of free-thinking hippies.

April, Ron sighed. If only he could let her go. But he loved her. And she had bested him by falling out of the car. He would get her back and never let her go again. It was only a matter of time.

Forty Three

Pulling up to Judith's house, Nicky smiled to herself. She remembered the last time she was here. Judith had told her she looked like a feral cat, and she did. But everything was different this time. Or it should be. However, she couldn't shake the uneasy feeling that Ron was near. How could he be?

Cindy was already out of her car and waiting for her at the door. "Ready to meet Ginny?"

"Ready as I'll ever be."

"We're in the kitchen," Judith called out as they knocked on the storm door. The main door was wide open and unlocked.

Nicky wondered why Judith was being so careless about who she invited into the house, but then she saw Judith had a view of her front door on the small screen sitting in front of her.

Seeing Nicky glance at it, Judith said, "Can't be too careful these days."

Nodding in agreement, Nicky smiled at April, and got a wan smile in return. And then she turned her gaze to Ginny.

Ginny smiled too, but it didn't reach her eyes, although she crinkled them up to make it look like it did.

"Hi, I'm Ginny, April's friend. I've heard so much about you. You're the one that found out about Ron Page, aren't you?"

Nicky waited a beat before answering, wondering if she enjoyed being identified that way. She had the fleeting thought that perhaps she needed to decide exactly how she wanted to be known. Now that Sara was safe, it was time to think about what she wanted before Sara went missing.

But all that flashed by in a second as she stared at Ginny. She had seen her before, but where?

"I know you from somewhere," Nicky blurted out.

"I doubt it," Ginny said and then held her breath, hoping it was true that Nicky had never seen her before and didn't know who she was.

"Probably not then," Nicky responded, but everyone at the table knew she still thought she had.

"Well, I'll leave you all to it," Ginny said. "I have a book I have been meaning to read. Nice to meet you, Nicky."

Judith waited until she heard Ginny's door close before looking at Nicky and saying, "What?"

Nicky shook her head and whispered, "I know I have seen her before."

"I think we agree she isn't who she appears to be. Booker is checking her out."

Judith didn't add that she had her internet expert, Matt, doing the same thing. For now, she wanted to keep Matt's existence to herself. Matt enjoyed being invisible, and she enjoyed having him as a secret weapon.

She also didn't add that she had attempted to confront Ginny earlier and failed to get any useful information. Partly because she didn't want to push Ginny too hard, and partly because Ginny was good at side stepping confrontation. And that was why she had asked Matt for help.

"You are worried, though, aren't you?" April asked Nicky. "It's why you came to Spring Falls."

"Yes. And to make sure you are doing okay."

April sighed. She was growing weary of the focus on her and who she used to be. She was no longer Ron's wife. She was her own person, and she was going to make a new life without him, and the last thing she wanted was to be identified by what happened to her. But she understood why Nicky needed to be reassured.

"You are not responsible for who Ron is and what he did. And I am profoundly grateful that you showed me the truth. Didn't—don't like it, but I am free now, and you are largely responsible for that."

Nicky's eyes filled with tears and April stood up and pulled Nicky up to hug her. Cindy and Judith watched with tears in their eyes, too.

"Hey," April said, "Let's go look at the house. I want your advice on what to do with it. We never got to do that last time you were here. And maybe Marsha could join us. It's time to get her dance/theater school up and running."

But when they called her, Marsha said she was staying in the hospital, so it was just Nicky and April who went to the house. Ron watched them leave, only slightly tempted to snatch April now. But he stopped himself. It wasn't time. He had a plan, and the quick snatch was not part of it. It was not dramatic or final enough.

Both Ginny and Ron knew where each Ruby Sister went after that. Cindy went home, and Bree returned from the woods, went to see Booker at the police station, and then they went out to dinner together. But Ginny didn't much care. She wanted to do some research on the Harry person.

Ron cared. April and the Ruby Sisters were now his entire focus. So he followed April and Nicky to the house. His house that he bought for his wife, who didn't stick by him when he needed her. He felt himself tense up in anger and quickly shut it down. Anger made people stupid, and that was something he never intended to be again.

He was determined, not angry. He was full of vengeance, but not angry. To Ron, they were entirely different emotions. One made mistakes, the others didn't. *It's not time yet,* he reminded himself, *but it's getting close.* First, he wanted them all to worry, be afraid, and feel nervous. Ginny was seeing to that.

That evening, when everyone was tucked away in their own house, he texted Ginny, asking how she was doing.

"All is going according to plan," she responded. She didn't tell him that nobody liked her. She didn't tell him she had another plan that involved Marsha and her father. And she didn't tell him that Nicky had recognized her.

As much as Ginny admired and cared about Ron Page, she knew he was a madman. That he was dangerous only made the game more fun for her. And to get away with what she wanted to do, she had to keep him dangling.

She knew what Ron wanted, and she'd give it to him. But she'd get what she wanted out of it, too.

Forty Four

While everyone else slept, Ginny worked. She didn't need anything to keep her awake. Hyped up and strung as tightly as a guitar string, Ginny couldn't have slept even if she wanted to.

She might not be a planner and organized, but when she was ready to do something, she did it well. And now she was ready. Her eavesdropping had paid off. Now she knew who had been in the black car and was now in the hospital.

Sitting cross-legged on her bed, she searched the internet for everything she could find out about Harry Harrison. It was surprisingly little. Everything she read was about him, not by him. He had earned the nickname the Hawk, not by being a predator, but by spotting them. In the business world. There was nothing about his private life.

Ginny knew how hard it was to remain invisible in today's world. It took more than Harry staying off social media. It took skill and a lot of work to have so little known about himself and the workings of his businesses. Ginny mentally saluted Harry for that ability.

But it meant she'd have to call in some favors and use some of her sources to dig into his business and personal life. She wanted to uncover something juicy and preferably scandalous. He had to have done something wrong somewhere.

But what was both surprising and delightful was that there was no mention anywhere that he was dying. And that he was in Spring Falls to meet his daughter. She couldn't imagine how he had kept it secret, but now she knew and it would no longer be a secret.

This was the scoop that would change her life. She and only she had this story. All she had to do was sell it to the highest bidder. She just wasn't sure where to start.

Ginny wanted nothing she knew to leak out before she got the full story. It was one reason she hesitated. Maybe she should write the story first. Or bribe Harry first for not publishing it.

That was another option. But he had to wake up if that was going to happen and that wasn't a sure thing. Either way, by selling the story, or bribing Harry to not print it, she had hit the jackpot.

And then there was the other story she had already sold. The Ron Page story. She was the only one who could tell this story, too.

Life had not been fair to her in the past, but now, it was making it up to her big time. If she had never gone to work for Ron Page, this would never have happened. *It's funny how life twists around before rewarding you,* Ginny thought.

She was shocked when she got the first phone call from Ron. And excited. So he had noticed her, after all. Of course, she had read about what he was and had been doing, but that didn't worry her.

After following him years before, she had seen it, and to her credit, kept it to herself. But now that it was out in the open, he was fair game. And he apparently only hunted strangers, and she wasn't a stranger anymore. Besides, it wasn't her he wanted. It was April and her friends.

When Ron explained he wanted her to find April on her travels, become her friend, and then go to Spring Falls and bring April and her friends to him, she had thought it was impossible.

But Ron had made an irresistible offer. He'd pay her, and then, when it was all over, they could be together. Plus, she knew she could then write the story of what happened.

Ginny knew Ron wasn't stupid. He would know she would write the story. She thought that perhaps since the fame he had ignored all his life had now found him, he now wanted more. That was an angle she would explore in the story.

Even if all of this went to hell in a handbasket, she still had a story. But if she could drag it out until it was almost too late, it would make it even better. Ginny giggled to herself. No one else in the world would ever have the chance to do what Ron had offered her.

Besides, she was not actually going to turn April and her friends over to Ron. She wasn't a good person, but she also wasn't that evil. It was why she was acting so obnoxious. Well, Ginny knew she wasn't that nice, anyway, so it was easy and fun to be so rude to the Ruby Sisters. Especially Judith.

Ginny knew Judith would question what she was up to. Maybe do a little research on her. But they wouldn't find much. She wrote and traveled under many names. Whatever suited her fancy.

This time she had used her real name because people needed to know the person who wrote the story. However, when Judith looked, she still wouldn't find much about her, which was good. Judith would trust her even less, and that's what Ginny wanted.

Because when Ron put his plan into action, which included her setting them up, they wouldn't trust her. And she wanted them to talk together to figure out what was happening. And by listening in, she would have even more information for her story. Information that no one but her would ever discover about them.

Ginny could envision the story now. How she uncovered Ron Page's plan to capture his wife and hurt her friends. That's what he had told her he was going to do, and she believed him.

But she had no intention of letting it go that far. Before he arrived in Spring Falls, she'd tell the truth. They would capture Ron. She would be safe and famous for her reporting work.

And then, the fabulous story about Harry the Hawk had been dumped right into her lap. She already had a contract for the Ron story. *Should she go to the same source and sell the Harry story? Did she care that the Ruby Sisters would never speak to her again?* Absolutely not. They were too goody-two-shoes for her, anyway.

By morning, Ginny had decided. She would turn in the story about Harry and tell Ron Page's plan to Bree's friend Booker. It was handy that he was the police chief and that she had met him.

She could make a deal with him, to protect herself from Ron, and with the money Ron had paid her to do this work, and what she would earn from her stories about Ron and about Harry and his daughter, she'd be home free.

And after that, no more playing these games, Ginny told herself. *Write good stories. Maybe write a book.* That she had already alienated the people who might have been able to help her didn't bother her. In fact, she wasn't sure if she could keep that agreement with herself anyway.

She enjoyed playing games, and she also liked that she wasn't always a good person. But that wouldn't stop her from writing that good book. She had all the ingredients for it right here in Spring Falls.

Forty Five

Harry couldn't move. He was a prisoner inside his own body. But he heard everything. It was as if because all his other senses had deserted him, he could now hear better than he had ever heard before.

From the changing sounds, he knew it was almost morning. The soft sound of footsteps in the hall. The clicks, and buzzes of machines. People's voices coming from far away. Some sounds he didn't want to hear. Weeping. And pain.

Harry did his best to block those sounds out, but they would seep in, making him want to get up and help, and he couldn't. He couldn't move anything. He and his body were not working together anymore. Never in his life had Harry felt so frustrated and helpless. There were important things he still had to do.

Of course, he could hear the sounds coming from his room. The hum of the instruments that were keeping him alive, and he was sure he heard a creature moving in the walls, probably a mouse.

But what comforted him was that he could hear the soft snoring that he would recognize anywhere. It was Amir watching over him, as he had done for so many years. And he knew there were two more people in the room. The sounds of people he loved in his room filled his heart with joy.

Bruce didn't snore, but every once in a while he shifted and groaned in his chair. Harry smiled to himself. He knew how hard it was to sleep in a chair. He had done it many times, mostly unintentionally, working too hard and long into the night.

Why had he done that? Why had he worked so hard? Harry knew the answer. It was simple. He liked what he was doing. He wanted to do good in the world, and too many wealthy people hadn't made that choice. He did. He would be wealthy and he'd do good. And he had.

Only a few trusted advisers knew what he was doing. But there was only one person who knew everything. The one person no one would expect—his driver. Amir knew it all. It was Amir who held all his secrets. And that was a secret, too. One they both kept, and that Harry treasured.

When Amir had started as a driver, he was young, inexperienced, and trying to support his family. And that was the way it had been for the first year. Amir did his job, and Harry kept quiet. But although he was happy, Harry was also lonely, though he had rarely admitted that, even to himself.

Well, he rarely admitted the happy part either. Partly because he wanted people to know him as calculating but fair. A stoic. A loner who did what he said, and could be trusted.

Harry wanted to make the world a better place, but not to become important himself. Harry didn't want people to know him as happy. He wanted them to be slightly afraid of him, because it was fear in all its forms that often made things happen.

When Harry felt angry at the injustices of the world, which were a daily occurrence now, it made him happy that he had the resources to do what he could about it. If he could describe himself, he would say he was a warrior for right. Like Marsha's friend Judith.

Even when Judith was a young girl, he had felt a kinship with her. And over the years, his admiration for her grew. She fought for what was right too, out in the open, unlike him, who worked behind the scenes. He was profoundly grateful for Judith, and for the other Ruby Sisters who watched out for his daughter.

Over the years, he had made many wrong decisions, and had done what he could to correct them. But the decision he had made agreeing to Marsha's mother's request was the one he now knew was the worst wrong one. And he still hadn't fixed that one, and he had to.

Harry knew he should have tried much sooner, but it had taken him many years to accept that being gay did not make him a bad person, and that he wouldn't ruin his daughter's life by being in it. And to realize that breaking his promise to Marsha's mother was the right thing to do.

As Harry lay still, he thought about his life. Yes, he had found happiness in his work, and yes, he had been lonely. He hadn't known that what he needed was a friend. And he never would have expected that the friend would be the young man who had become his driver.

One day, Harry had talked and Amir had listened. It had taken many years, but eventually Harry had told Amir everything, trusting him to keep it all to himself. And he had.

That Amir was waiting by the side of his bed for him to wake didn't surprise Harry at all. But he still wanted to tell him again how grateful he was for Amir's friendship. A friendship that had become so much more.

And he knew Amir was still waiting for further instructions on the plan the two of them had set up. Both of them knew he had to wake up long enough to set it in motion.

Now, listening to the sounds of the room, unable to move or wake up, he could also hear the soft sounds of his daughter's breathing. Yesterday he had listened as she had told him about her life, and who she was, and what she was, and he hadn't been able to move to thank or comfort her.

Harry was more frustrated than he could remember ever being. He had accepted his death, planned everything out so everyone was taken care of, including Marsha. But he wanted to talk to her. And he needed to make sure that Amir had everything in place.

And he was helpless. He was aware and awake and yet he was not. He could feel danger surrounding Marsha and her friends. Did they know it? Were they doing anything about it?

He groaned, but he knew the sound never came out. It was all inside of him. Maybe that was the biggest mistake he had made in life, keeping so many things inside of him, and not making more friends.

I did my best, Harry said to himself. *But I need to talk to Marsha and Amir. And Bruce, my new friend.* He needed to tell Bruce to not keep secrets.

Yes, Harry thought, *I have more to say before I go.* But for once, he did not know how to accomplish something. Maybe the most important thing in his life. He did not know how to wake up.

Forty Six

Nicky couldn't sleep either.

After Ginny went to her room, Nicky told Judith, Cindy, and April, that she was sure she had seen Ginny before. She just couldn't remember where.

The three of them talked for a while longer about Marsha and Harry, and made plans to take Rachel and Bryan to Harry as soon as they arrived in the morning.

Then Nicky drove April to the Ruby House to see what Marsha and Seth had accomplished while she was away. The maple tree had leafed out, and a crow flew past the car up into the tree as they drove into the newly paved driveway and new parking lot. They both thought the crow was welcoming them, and they waved to it as they went in the front door.

Opening the door, they stood in astonishment. The wood floor gleamed. The windows were new and sparkling. Light filtering through the maple tree cast shadows on the newly painted dove gray walls.

April's reaction was pure delight. As they walked through the house, Nicky smiled at the way April gawked at everything around her, her mouth hanging open and her eyes wide as she took in the rooms. She oohed and aahed, and squeezed Nicky's hand excitedly, letting out an occasional "Oh my god!" or "I can't believe how beautiful it is!"

Nicky walked beside April as she pointed at things and talked through what she thought they would do. With each room inspection, April's voice sounded more and more like the April she had first met.

The elevator that Marsha had suggested had been installed and only after seeing it did April realize what a brilliant suggestion it had been. Now, when they worked on the upstairs, it would be so much easier to bring up the equipment and supplies they needed.

Nicky asked April to explain all that she wanted to do, partially because she was interested, but even more because she loved seeing the spark of delight in April's eyes.

By the time they had finished the tour, April was almost like the April she had met a few months before. And whatever tension had been between them because of Ron had dissipated.

Finally, April plopped herself down in the middle of the empty downstairs space, imagining what could happen there. It felt as if the house was waiting with joyful expectancy to be something again.

Like me, April thought.

"My offer is still here, Nicky. If you'd like to be part of the redesigning of this house, just say the word."

Nicky's heart felt as if it would burst with happiness. But she had explained to April that her place was still with Sara, as Sara healed. And she promised she would be back to celebrate with them all when they finished the Ruby House.

When April asked Nicky how long she was planning to stay in town this time, and she answered she was staying until she was sure that April and the rest of the Ruby Sisters were safe, April had responded with a simple thank you.

Nicky felt the depth of meaning behind the words and felt another layer of guilt melt away.

Neither of them had seen Ron watching the house. Even if they had, they wouldn't have recognized him.

Despite that, Nicky knew something was wrong. And until she figured out what it was, she wasn't going anywhere. She was glad that Judith had given the directive that April couldn't go anywhere by herself.

After dropping April off at Judith's, she returned to Cindy's. She and Cindy had a quiet dinner together and headed off to bed. It had been a day of revelations and turmoil, and they were both exhausted.

Except now, hours later, almost morning, Nicky was wide awake. Worrying. Not even sure what she was worrying about. But since she couldn't sleep, she decided to go see Marsha. Since Marsha had rushed off to the hospital, neither she nor Cindy had talked to her.

Maybe that's all that's bothering me, Nicky thought.

So Nicky left a note for Cindy in case she woke up wondering where she was, and drove to the hospital, all the time wondering if it was a good idea. Would Marsha want her there? What good could she do?

But she went anyway. She knew that Bryan and Rachel would be there in the morning, and she wanted to be with Marsha when they came. However, when Nicky arrived at the hospital, she was told there were too many people in the room, and she couldn't go in unless someone left.

While trying to decide what to do, she looked up and saw Marsha heading down the hall and rushed after her.

"What are you doing here?" Marsha asked, startled.

"I thought I would come and wait with you. If you don't mind, that is."

Marsha looked away, thinking she would rather be alone, and then realized that wasn't true. That was the old Marsha. Nicky knew all her secrets and yet still wanted to be friends.

What a mess I've made, Marsha thought.

"I'd love it," Marsha said. "I was heading to the dining room for coffee. Would you like to join me?"

Nicky looked up at Marsha and smiled. Despite the bags under her eyes, and her face showing the tension she was feeling, Nicky thought Marsha was one of the most beautiful people she had ever seen.

For Marsha's part—standing in the hospital's hall, hating every smell and beep that surrounded them—for the first time in her life, she allowed herself to be seen by someone else.

It wasn't a conscious decision. Maybe it happened because Nicky had heard her secret and still was there for her. Or her now burning desire to talk to her father before he died.

Whatever it was, it had opened a door that had been closed her entire life. She waited, trembling, wondering what Nicky was seeing.

Then Nicky smiled, her face lighting up in delight, and Marsha felt as if she had come home.

Forty Seven

Bryan and Rachel left before dawn. Both of them loved being up and about before the world woke up, but that wasn't the reason they left so early. Bryan couldn't sleep. He felt an undeniable urge to get to Spring Falls as soon as possible, and as much as he tried to tell himself to ignore it, he couldn't.

He was worried, but didn't understand why. He felt the itch of something going on and that he was supposed to be helping right at that moment. Knowing Bree was an early riser, Rachel had texted her, saying they were on their way. Should they go to her house first, or the hospital?

When Bree didn't answer—and although Bryan knew it was possible Bree was still sleeping—it raised his anxiety level to where Rachel couldn't stand it anymore and insisted that she drive. Although Bryan protested at first, seeing his hands shake on the wheel, he agreed. They pulled into an empty parking lot and switched places. Bryan wasn't sure that helped much. He still felt like ants were crawling up his arm. But Rachel assured him they weren't, and besides, she felt better now that she was driving.

"Try sleeping," she suggested. "I'm sure everyone else is still sleeping. We can text Judith and Bree right before we get there and let them know we are going straight to the hospital. Or perhaps try reaching Harry now? While I drive, you can do your thing."

For a moment Bryan thought about what other people might think if they overheard their conversation, or if they knew he was going to find a man in a coma and talk to him.

It was absurd, really. Even he thought so sometimes. How normal was it that his days were often filled with the people no one else saw? He called them the people in the in-between.

It wasn't the life Bryan thought he would be living. And if he could, he'd choose to be something more ordinary, like maybe a gardener. Whatever it was, it couldn't keep him inside. His ordinary job would have to be outside. And although he did garden, it wasn't his work. Helping people in the in-between was.

What he did was something he rarely shared with people, because even he had trouble believing it sometimes. Still, what could he do? The people were there, imaginary or not, and he had to help.

However, without Rachel, he was fairly sure he would have gone crazy by now. Although some people might say that he was crazy already, Rachel assured him he wasn't. Sometimes she saw the people, too, when she held onto him and he opened up the way for her.

So they were either crazy together, or it was really happening. Either way, they were together, and that's what counted. And he felt he was doing a good thing in the world. And that counted even more.

So he closed his eyes and did what Rachel suggested and looked for Harry. And a few minutes later, he found him.

• • • • ● • ● ● ● • •

Ginny had decided. She would go to the police station and tell Booker her story. Privately. But only after getting his assurance that not only would she not be prosecuted for her role in Ron's plan, but ask for and get protection from him. At least until they found and arrested Ron and put him behind bars forever. Then she'd be safe.

In the meantime, she'd publish her story about Ron. And she would tell her favorite paper about the Harry story and get paid for that too. The only reason she hadn't tried to sell Harry's story yet is she knew too little, and she was hoping to interview Marsha and Harry if he woke up.

Even if they both said no, it was still a story.

In the meantime, she needed to get away from Ron. During the night, as she wrote the story, she had an epiphany. After getting his text, she had a moment of panic. It was not something she had felt before.

Usually she was fearless, or at least that's what she told herself. But that moment of panic had forced her to stop and think. It was only then that she admitted to herself that she had been fooling herself about Ron wanting to be with her. She had always known that for Ron, April was all there was.

But what had really shifted for her in the night was the realization that she didn't want him either. The whole "I want Ron" thing had been all about conquest. Winning. And although she lost the battle on the relationship front, it was minor compared to what she would win by exposing him.

Looking at her nails where she had been biting them again this last week, despite her determination not to, she knew what she had to do. She was in over her head. She had to get help and that would be Booker.

Hoping Booker was an early riser, but at least figuring that the police station would be open, Ginny packed her bag, and as silently as possible, slipped out of Judith's house.

At the last minute, Ginny did something she thought she'd never do. She trusted someone. She copied her story about Ron and all her notes to a thumb drive and left it on the dresser in her room with a note to Judith, saying that she was trusting her to never look at it unless something happened to her.

That she was leaving something behind just in case, astonished Ginny. Was she that afraid? Did she trust Judith to not look?

Yes, Ginny thought. *I actually am that afraid. And I think I trust Judith. But right now, I don't have any other choice.*

She cared about winning. Ron cared about satisfaction and vengeance. It was that awareness as she wrote her story that had made her decide to get help.

Stepping out of the door into the predawn, she looked around. Was Ron in town and she didn't know it? She hoped not.

Now trembling, she slipped into her car and headed to the police station, hoping she hadn't waited too long. Not to do what was right—that wasn't important to her—but too long before getting protection from a crazy man.

Forty Eight

Booker was standing at the front desk staring out the window, wondering why he was at work so early when he didn't have to be when he saw Ginny running toward the station.

Putting his coffee down, he rushed to the door and Ginny practically fell into his arms as he opened it.

"Are you alright?"

Ginny shook her head, the red streak in her dark hair flashing as she did so.

"Can you lock the door?" Ginny asked, panting in fear.

For Booker it was a bit too much, and as soon as Ginny realized her act didn't impress him, she stopped the panting and the frenzied look and asked, "Not buying it?"

"Nope. What is this act all about?"

Before Ginny had a chance to answer, the door opened and Nicky walked in. Seeing Ginny, she said, "I remembered where I saw you before, Ginny, and I came to tell Booker about it. And your name wasn't Ginny then."

"It took you long enough."

Booker smiled to himself as he watched Nicky step forward, no longer the scared woman from just a few months ago. Now she looked ready to fight, and for a moment, he was worried about Ginny.

Stepping between the two women, he said, "Let's go into my office and you two can tell me what this is all about."

Glaring at Ginny, Nicky led the way into the office, recalling the last time she had been here. It seemed like a hundred years before, but they were still dealing with the same problem. Ron Page was still causing havoc by playing with people's lives.

Booker was thinking the same thing. This was about Ron Page. Stopping at the front desk to speak to his assistant, he leaned over so only she could hear and said, "Get in touch with all the Ruby Sisters. Find out where they are. Tell them to either come here or go someplace that they all can be together. Then assign an officer to that place."

Once Booker confirmed that all his instructions were carried out, he returned to his office, where he found Nicky and Ginny sitting as far apart from each other as they could. Nicky looked as if she were ready to punch Ginny, while Ginny tried to appear as if she didn't care. But her face was pale, and she was working hard to keep her hands still in her lap.

"What's this all about, ladies?" Booker asked, after getting coffee for them both.

"Ron," they said together.

Before they had a chance to explain, Booker's assistant opened the door, and he stepped outside to hear what she had to say, closing the door behind him.

"Judith and April are on the way to the station. Cindy is going to the hospital to be with Marsha, and an officer is heading there to be with them. But I can't reach Bree. What do you want me to do?"

Booker tried not to let the panic he felt show, because even though logic told him it was probably nothing, his gut said otherwise. Bree was always awake by now.

"Send an officer to her house and bring her here. Then send someone to her daughter's house to make sure they are okay."

Sending an officer to Mary's is probably unnecessary, Booker thought. He was probably overreacting. He doubted Ron wanted anything to do with his daughter. But he might use Mary and her family to get to April.

Yes, he was erring on the side of caution, but in this case, lives could be at stake. Taking a deep breath, he returned to the office to find out what Ginny and Nicky could tell him. Just hearing Ron's name had made every cell in his body tingle. He'd find him, but first he had to make sure everyone was safe.

Judith got the call while looking out at her garden. She was watching the sun turn the clouds red, making her think of the saying, "Red skies in the morning, sailors take warning. Red sky at night, sailor's delight."

Although she wasn't a sailor, Judith felt as if the red sky this morning was telling her something. And when she saw the call coming through from the police station, she knew she was right.

She told the officer that Marsha would not leave the hospital and asked her to please send someone there. She'd get April and come to the police station.

On the way to wake April, Judith saw Nicky's note and the fear she had felt before tripled. She grabbed the note and the thumb drive and stuck them in her pocket. April was already awake and almost dressed when Judith rushed in. April's face paled, and her knees gave way, forcing her back to the bed.

"It's Ron, isn't it?"

"I don't know. I only know that Ginny is gone and Booker wants us to come to the police station."

At the hospital, Marsha got the phone call from Cindy, who said she was on her way to be with her. Marsha thought the world had gone mad. Nicky had said, "I know where I saw that woman," before rushing out the door, but had turned around and kissed Marsha on the check before leaving.

Marsha could still feel the kiss. What did it mean? But with Cindy's call, all that was washed away. Rushing to her father's room, she told Bruce and Amir that something was happening.

"Something is happening here, too," Bruce said, gesturing to Harry.

Marsha looked at her father, hoping for a miracle. Although his body was as still as ever, his eyes were moving behind his eyelids.

"What's going on?" Marsha asked, rushing to her father's bedside.

"I think he's talking to someone," Amir said.

Outside the police station, Ron laughed to see the flurry Ginny and Nicky's arrival had caused. Nicky had been a surprise, but a good one. It made for even more drama. It was interesting to watch them scurry around like ants whose rock had been pulled away, exposing them to the world.

Usually Ron enjoyed acting privately, not showing his hand, and definitely not alerting people to his presence. He had enjoyed the quiet hunt. The silent kill.

But this time, he had planned something a little more flamboyant. And he had discovered that he loved it. So he'd let the play go on. But once he accomplished his goal—to force April to come and stay with him—he'd go back to being the invisible predator.

For now, though, he found this excitement over him thrilling. Too bad they didn't know what he knew. That the trap had already been set, and he had the bait in his car, bound and tied in the trunk.

Booker would have to let April go. He'd trade her for Bree any day.

Forty Nine

Bryan and Harry were talking. Not the way they would speak to each other if they were both in their bodies. Bryan knew he could never really explain to anyone else what was happening since he could barely explain it to himself. They were speaking unbound by the material sense of the world and meeting somewhere else.

Where that somewhere else was, Bryan didn't know. He simply had to accept that it was possible, and let someone else explain how it was happening.

At first Harry was afraid. *As he should be,* Bryan thought. Bryan could be anyone trying to control him. Or hurt him.

But Bryan assured him he was there to help and showed him his memories of the last time he had been in Spring Falls with the Ruby Sisters.

"You know my daughter?"

"Your daughter?"

"Marsha, my daughter."

Bryan took a beat before answering that he did, even though that was news to him, and added that he was looking forward to seeing the changes that she and April had made in the Ruby House.

That answer assured Harry enough to ask Bryan what he wanted.

It impressed Bryan. Harry would not waste anytime trying to figure out how this was happening. He was going straight to the issue.

As quickly as he could, Bryan explained the situation. Bree had asked him to come see Harry. Helping people in the in-between was something he did, and he had helped the Ruby Sisters once before. She thought he could help Harry return to his body.

"Or leave it altogether," Harry said, clarifying to Bryan that Harry did grasp what was going on.

"Or leave it. Either way, I am here for you now."

Rachel glanced over at Bryan, who looked as if he was asleep, but she knew he wasn't. She could see his eyes moving behind his closed eyelids. Thinking that he needed to know, she whispered they were about forty-five minutes away.

Bryan smiled to himself. It had been the question Harry had just asked him.

"Not soon enough," Harry said. "I need to speak to Amir."

Once Harry told him who Amir was, and what he wanted him to tell him, Bryan said he'd see Harry soon, and closed the connection. He could feel how much the contact had taken out of Harry and he would need all his strength to return to his body if that was what he really wanted to do.

Besides, it had drained him, too. He needed to recover if he was going to be of any use.

After taking a drink of water, Bryan dialed the number that Harry had given him.

At the hospital, Harry's eyes had stopped moving and Amir felt a stab of fear. He looked at Marsha, hoping she knew what was happening. Was it all over? What had been going on? Would they ever know?

At that moment Amir's phone rang, startling him. No one knew the phone number except Harry. But Harry was lying in front of him, looking even frailer than before, if that were possible.

Not knowing what to do, Amir let the phone go to voice mail. And then it rang again. In his head, he thought he heard Harry say, "answer it." Thinking it was a lack of sleep and an abundance of worry that was causing a hallucination, he hesitated.

Finally, not being able to stand it any longer, Amir answered, grimacing with worry. Not saying anything. Waiting for what was going to happen. He half expected it to be Harry calling him, which was impossible, of course. But although it wasn't Harry, it was Harry's words.

The man on the phone said it was impossible to explain what was happening, but to please believe him, and then he used a code word that only Amir and Harry knew. So, despite feeling as if he had stepped into crazy land, Amir did what the man asked him to do—what Harry was asking him to do. Stepping out into the hall, he made the phone call Harry had told him to make.

Then he prayed for two things. That they weren't too late, and that the man coming to the hospital could bring his friend back to him. Just a few minutes more was all he asked. For himself, for Harry's daughter, and Harry's new friend, Bruce. They all needed a little more time to say goodbye in the proper way.

Amir unconsciously patted his jacket pocket where Harry's envelope and instructions were, right over his heart, where they were safe.

Bruce had watched Harry's eyes go still and thought he knew what was happening. He had witnessed what Bryan could do when Bryan brought April back and then let them watch as Paul moved into the light. He sat down by the bed and held Harry's hand, hoping to pass some of his strength to his friend.

When Marsha saw Harry's eyes go still, she was afraid that meant it was over. She would never get to tell Harry that she was remembering all the times she had seen him. Not that she had known who he was. But she had seen him. A man that had been at all her performances, her graduation, and sometimes outside the school. Once she had glimpsed him in the crowd at one of her performances in New York.

When they were in school, all the Ruby Sisters had seen the man who looked so happy to be there. But they thought he was someone's father. Well, now she knew. It was someone's father. Hers. And she was tired of holding it against him for not being there for her. He had been.

On the other side of the bed from Bruce, Marsha held Harry's other hand, asked him to come back, even if just for a little while.

She heard Amir's phone ring and watched him step out of the room. And then Bruce's phone rang, and he stepped out of the room too.

I don't want to know, Marsha said to herself. *I just can't stand one more bad thing happening.*

But a few minutes later, when Cindy rushed into the room, Marsha knew that whatever was happening was very bad, and she had a decision to make. Would she face it, or retreat again, back into herself, covered in cotton padding, so life would not be so loud or so hard? Or would she be the daughter and friend she wanted to be?

Choose now, she said to herself. And then she did.

Fifty

Booker stood in the doorway of his office, looking at Ginny and Nicky. What he wanted to do was storm in and shake Ginny until her teeth rattled, but knew that would never get him the answers he needed.

Inside the station, the air felt heavy. *There is a rainstorm coming,* he thought. The weight of all that was happening pressed down on Booker, his fear for Bree screaming at him to do something. Anything.

But Booker knew if he showed his anger and his fear, he'd get nothing out of Ginny. She was here for a reason. And he needed to find out now what it was. Booker knew Ginny was playing games, but playing games with Ron was a deadly thing to be doing.

For a moment, Booker allowed himself to think about Bree. They had dinner, had a lovely time together as they always did, as friends. But then, as he dropped her off at her house, without thinking, he had leaned in and kissed her. And she kissed him back. Briefly, then turned and went inside, closing the door behind her. But the kiss had lasted long enough for him to know that the spark they had felt in high school was still present. And he wanted more. And now she was missing.

Booker wished he had brought his dog, Addie, with him to the office today. She would have kept him calm. He'd have to pretend she was there because he needed all the calmness and courage he could gather to find Bree and keep everyone safe.

Taking a deep breath, he brushed his hair away from his face, reminding himself he needed a haircut when this was over, and stepped into the room. Nicky continued to stare at Ginny, her arms crossed, chin jutting forward, blue eyes blazing while Ginny slouched in the other chair, avoiding Nicky's piercing glare.

Crossing his arms and glaring at Ginny, Booker then turned to Nicky and asked, "Okay, how do you know this woman?"

Nicky stood up and walked over to stand beside Booker, while continuing to glare at Ginny, who tried to glare back and failed. To Ginny's dismay, her bottom lip quivered. Ginny tried to remind herself that she had this all under control. All she wanted was a story. They'd understand that, wouldn't they?

"I saw her walking with Ron in Spring Falls during the time I was watching him. A few years ago. More than once. At first I was worried for her, knowing Ron. But by then, it was obvious he had learned to stay away from harming people he knew. I checked and learned that she worked for him at his financial firm. But her name was different and her hair was blonder and shorter then so I didn't recognize her."

"It's not what you think. I only worked for him in his office. I didn't work with him while he did his other stuff."

"But you knew what he did?" Booker demanded, hiding the fury that he felt. How could people allow such evil? Booker swallowed hard and looked at the floor, afraid of what he would say. *Stay calm,* he told himself.

Ginny dropped her head. There was no need to answer. Booker reached into his desk and pulled out a pair of handcuffs.

Ginny blanched, "Wait. That's what I'm here for. To tell you what's happening. I'm here to help."

"Well, you can help handcuffed to the chair, so you don't get any crazy ideas about leaving. And yes, you can start talking. Right now. And leave nothing out. It's the only chance you have of avoiding a lifetime in prison."

If it were possible, Ginny's face turned even whiter, and tears filled her eyes. She willed them not to drop. *She was in the right here, couldn't they see that?*

Looking at Nicky's steely gaze and feeling Booker's contained fury, she realized that they didn't. And for the first time, Ginny wondered if she had been wrong about the whole thing.

While reading Ginny her rights, Booker took out his cell phone and pressed the record button. It wasn't official, but it would have to do for now.

"Prison?" Ginny squeaked out. "I didn't do anything."

Leaning in over her chair, his face directly in front of Ginny's, Booker hissed his questions through clenched teeth. Ginny started trembling. Just as he wanted her to. He wanted her to be more afraid of him than of Ron.

"You are not that stupid. You know you did. Now start talking. I want to know everything. But what you need to know is Bree is missing, and until we find her safe and sound, you have no leverage at all. I want you to tell me right now what you know. Is Ron Page in town? Does he have Bree? Where is he?"

"Bree's missing?"

Booker looked away from Ginny and saw Judith standing in the doorway, her face pale and like him, her hands clinched in fists.

"Judith, this is a private office. You can't just walk in here," Booker said, and then, seeing Judith's face, realized he couldn't stop her. And maybe she could help.

Without waiting for Booker's answer, Judith strode in and stood in front of Ginny's chair, delighted to see Bruce had handcuffed her to it, and stared.

Nicky thought that if Judith stared at her like that, she'd tell her everything. Between Booker and Judith, Ginny was toast.

Then she heard a whimper and looked up to see April leaning against the door, looking as if she would collapse. Gathering her in her arms, Nicky guided April to a chair. Seeing a bottle of water on Booker's desk, she handed it to her, saying, "Drink this."

Hell's bells, Booker said to himself. You'd think I wasn't the person in charge here. Once again, his office was overrun with Ruby Sisters.

While he was trying to decide how much to allow Judith to talk to Ginny, his assistant gestured from the doorway. It took all his strength not to scream "what?" at her. Booker followed her into the hallway, leaving Judith glaring at Ginny and Nicky caring for April.

"A man is in the waiting room. I don't recognize him and he won't give me his name. He's demanding to speak to you. Right now."

"What does he want?"

"He just said it was about Ron Page."

Hope and fear flared equally in Booker. But he kept them both under control. Looking back into his office, he thought perhaps it was a good thing that two of the Ruby Sisters were there.

Stepping back into the room, he said, "Get the answers, Judith. Nicky, take care of April. And lock the door behind me. Don't open it unless it's me."

Booker paused in the hall, waiting to hear the door lock, and to make sure that he was thinking clearly before going to find out who the man was, and what he wanted, praying that the man wasn't working for Ron and was there to help, not harm.

But erring on the side of caution, he motioned to his assistant to leave the room. Whatever this was, he'd have to handle it on his own.

Fifty One

Ron watched from across the street as a man entered the police station. Someone he didn't know. Someone acting so casual it couldn't be real.

Besides, how many people go to the police station this early in the morning? And he was walking. Did he live in town? If he did, how come he'd never seen him before? If he didn't, where was his car? Was he walking so his car wasn't visible? And if that was the case, from whom was he hiding his car? Booker? Why?

Or what if this is all about me? Ron thought. *Maybe he knows I am here, and he's hiding it from me. It's possible. They now know Bree is missing, and they might suspect that I'm responsible.*

But until the moment Ginny walked into the station, they knew nothing. Only suspected. As I wanted them to. I wanted them to be afraid. Actually, I want them to be terrified. But no one could have known in advance that I had returned to Spring Falls, or recognized me even if they would have seen me.

All this went through Ron's mind as he watched, hidden behind the privet hedge in front of the house where he had been staying.

A house directly across the street from the police station. Well, not staying so much as taken over.

The owners, well, they wouldn't be talking, Ron smirked to himself. They were resting quietly in the basement, wrapped in plastic. He hadn't known how long he would stay, and he hadn't wanted to live with a smell, or alert anyone, before he was through with the house.

He had sent out a text from their phones, letting friends know they had taken a vacation. And when friends responded, he had answered that they were going to take a vacation from social media and phones, too. They'd see them soon.

All the heart emojis and good wishes they had responded with made him want to gag. Then he destroyed their phones. Not in a rage, although he had wanted to, but quietly and methodically as he had always done. Managing his emotions had made his businesses successful. Both of them. The one that made money, and the one that made him happy.

Watching Ginny think she was smarter than him had provided him with much needed entertainment. She was such a fool. It pleased him to watch her do what he wanted her to do while sealing her own fate at the same time. But she had served him well, keeping April safe on her travels and making The Ruby Sisters suspicious and fearful.

Stalking the Ruby Sisters had been the most fun he'd had in a long while. It was all so delicious, watching everyone looking for him, and he was literally right in front of them. But now, all his plans were wrapping up, and his new life with April was about to begin.

April was in the police station where he wanted her to be. He had taken Bree out of the trunk of the car, and now she was in the basement waiting for the end. Not wrapped up like the homeowners. She was the live bait. It was the only way it would work. And it would work. That he was sure of, because he knew what he was doing, and they were only guessing.

Ron felt a drop of rain and glanced up. He hadn't noticed the dark clouds moving in and that worried him. He had missed the weather change? In fact, he should have noticed the wind that had changed from a warm breeze to one with an edge in it.

Ah well, it's time to go inside anyway, Ron thought. He needed to get cleaned up. Which was going to be such a pleasure to do. He didn't enjoy looking like someone else and he couldn't wait to shave, take off the ridiculous wig, and change his clothes.

He had bought a suit that he would change into once he had April. He had decided that exchanging marriage vows again would be the perfect new beginning. Thinking ahead, as he always did, he had bought April a dress to wear. It was hanging beside his suit. Of course, they'd have to get away before that ceremony happened. But he had planned for that, too.

A small plane waited for them at the airport outside of town. It was a tiny airport, but that made it all the better. He had paid the pilot to wait. And threatened him, too. It amused Ron that threats always seemed to work better than anything else. A fear response was what it was. It seemed to stop the brain from thinking. Luckily, it was a response he didn't have. Although he was a little nervous about how this would go, he wasn't afraid.

Ginny was keeping them occupied in the police station. April was with her, just as he had planned she would be. Now all he had to do was make the exchange. He had witnessed the Booker and Bree kiss the night before, sealing the deal, so to speak, about what Booker would do to get Bree back.

It was all playing according to his plan. The angels were on his side.

Back in the house, keeping the lights off as he had all week, Ron shaved, changed clothes, brushed his teeth, and packed the car he had purchased with cash in another state, with another identity.

Looking down the cellar steps, he saw Bree still passed out from the drugs he had given her. Bree had been one of his early conquests. Not satisfying, though. It took him a while to realize that what he enjoyed was the dying part. And the hunt. And the game. Like the one he was playing now. He always won. He'd win again.

Ron didn't stand in the doorway long because, despite his caution about wrapping up the homeowners, there was a faint stink coming off of them. It was disgusting. Thank heavens it was almost time. New man in the police station or not. It wouldn't matter who he was in the end. Everything was in place.

April would do anything to save her friends. That he was sure about. She wouldn't be saving anything, really, but she didn't need to know that until they were long gone. Safe where no one would find them.

He locked the cellar door and nailed a board across it. "No getting out of this, Bree," Ron said to her, just in case she was awake enough to hear. "Too bad you won't be able to write this experience in your book. It would have made for a good one."

Ron hoped the rain held off. He didn't want it to put out the fire he was going to start before it did the damage he needed it to do. Perhaps he should start it in the basement instead of in the living room.

But that would mean he'd have to open that door again, and the smell would get on him. He didn't want April to be disgusted with him. No, it would have to work the way he had planned it to.

Pulling out one of his burner phones, Ron prepared to make the call he had been waiting to make since the moment he had crossed over the border to Canada.

The phone call that would ensure he would possess April once again, and everyone else would pay for what they had done by taking her away from him. Ginny had kept April safe, and now Ginny would do the last thing she would ever do for him or anyone else.

Fifty Two

B ruce slumped against the wall, feeling his heartbeat, his eyes closed, breathing in and out, in, out, in, out. Too fast. He continued to focus on his breath, the way Judith had taught him, trying to slow his heart rate down. She had told him it helped her when she wanted to rage at the world and do something. Box breathing, she had called it. Simple to do and remember.

And it helped. A little. But what Judith had told him on the phone had shaken him to the core. Bree was missing, and they were sure that Ron had her. How that could be didn't seem possible. What had they missed?

He heard a soft noise and opened his eyes. Marsha was standing next to him, looking calmer than he had seen her in days.

Taking Bruce's hand, Marsha said, "I'm sorry. I've only been thinking about me. Feeling sorry for myself. Angry that the world doesn't work the way I want it to. And all of you have been so patient with me despite always wondering how I'll behave."

Bruce grabbed Marsha's other hand, feeling his heart slow down a little more. "It's okay. It's been a tough year for everyone."

"And that's my point. For everyone, not just me. So I appreciate your graciousness, Bruce, but I haven't been pulling my weight and I intend to do that from now on. So, tell me what's happening. There is something else going on and it's more than Harry lying there in the bed, isn't it?"

Bruce closed his eyes again, finding himself completely unable, or maybe unwilling, to answer.

Judith had left it up to him whether to tell Cindy and Marsha now that Bree was missing, or wait until they found her, because she was sure that they would. But Bruce knew Judith was only saying that because she couldn't face the other scenario.

Before hanging up, Judith had said, "What can they do from there? It's better that Marsha stays with Harry. In fact, it's better that you all stay there where it's safe. A police officer is on his way just to make sure."

So, even though Judith had said he could decide, he knew she thought it was best to wait. But was it? How could he know which way was best? Besides, he was more tired than he had ever been in his life, and all his thinking felt muddled. And he hadn't realized the level of his exhaustion until Judith's phone call.

He had been by Harry's side for the last few days. And since Harry had come to town, he had been constantly on his mind. Worrying if Marsha would ever accept Harry. Worrying that he hadn't handled Harry's estate properly.

All that worrying, and now the unbelievable fear and worry that descended on him after hearing Judith's news, was too much.

And now he had to make a decision when he was ping-ponging between fear and anger. For the first time in his life, he fully understood why some people just give up and stop taking part in life.

Bruce sighed and opened his eyes and looked at Marsha. She looked exhausted too, but she was different. He couldn't put his finger on it, but it made his heart feel a little lighter. Gave him a jolt of hope, something he realized he had been missing the last few days.

Waiting for Bruce to answer, Marsha felt afraid, but tried not to let it show. She hadn't noticed how tired Bruce had become. She had been too busy worrying about what she wanted and how she wanted it to be and feeling sorry for herself. Well, that was over. Now, she was going to be the one Bruce and Harry could count on. And whoever else who needed her.

"Bruce, tell me, who called?"

Bruce looked down the hall and noticed that Amir was no longer there. Where did he go? How could he leave Harry at a time like this? Who had been on the phone and what did they say? Then he saw a police officer exit the elevator and head to Harry's room.

The decision had been made for him. Cindy and Marsha needed to know.

Fifty Three

Under Judith's probing questions, Ginny quickly crumbled. Judith knew that none of what Ginny was telling them would stand up in court, even though the recording would be helpful.

But at that moment, all that was important was finding Bree. So Judith kept probing and pushing until Ginny relented and finally told all that she knew. How she had known Ron. How much she had wanted to trap him into a relationship, but failed. He never gave her the time of day. So she gave up, left her job and started writing for newspapers as a roving reporter looking for a big story. It was a tiny sliver of a living but enough to sustain her and her desire for adventure.

Yes, she changed her name a few times, but it wasn't any different than using a pen name. At least not to her.

"But you said you knew what Ron was up to?" Judith said, "How could you know and not turn him in?"

Ginny chewed her lower lip before making the decision that telling the truth was probably the only thing that could save her now. "Honestly, I liked the idea that I could have a smidgen of control over him. And besides, how could I prove any of it?"

"That's total bull-shit and you know it," Nicky said. "Think how many women you might have saved by speaking up."

Ginny just stared back at the woman standing by April's side. How would she understand? She was old.

"Keep going," Judith said, glancing at Nicky and April. If she had a choice, she would not have had them in the room. Nicky was furious, and April had started silently crying, not saying anything, just letting the tears run down her face. That scared Judith. She wanted April to be furious, not defeated.

"Why did you befriend April?"

"Ron got in contact with me. How he found me, I don't know. I had left town and been traveling for ages."

Nicky and Judith glared, so she kept going.

"He asked me to befriend April while she was on her travels because he wanted to make sure she was safe."

"In return for what?"

"Well, two things. We could be together, although he made it clear it would be on the side because April was and would always be his wife and only love."

Ginny almost spit out those last words looking over at April, who, to her, looked older than the hills. All collapsed on herself. She wondered why Ron would choose April over her. Perhaps he was an idiot after all.

"And he told me I could write his story. An exclusive. Make a ton of money. Be famous. Get off the road and start living. I was to make friends with April, and then come to Spring Falls and make friends with you."

"Well, that failed," Nicky said, then stopped talking after Judith glared at her.

"No, it didn't. I knew making friends would take too long, so I made you all suspicious of me. You know what you all did then? You started talking and whispering among yourself. I learned more from listening to you all when you thought I wasn't around, or couldn't hear, than I would have if I would have made nicey-nicey with you."

"And then you came to the police station to tell us all about it? Makes no sense," Judith said. "Unless you are afraid of Ron and thought we could help."

Ginny dropped her head, her dark hair falling forward so that when she looked up again, one strand of hair covered one of her eyes. Shaking her head to dislodge it, she said, "Well, I'm not stupid. He thought I believed him when he said he would be with me. I knew he was lying. But I wanted the story. And I wanted to be where the action would take place. Which is right here, isn't it, April?"

April reached into her purse, took out her phone, opened her text messages, and handed it to Judith to read. Three short words. "You, for Bree."

"Absolutely not," Judith said, keeping the phone and turning back to Ginny. "You brought us all here, didn't you? That was part of the plan, wasn't it?"

"Ding, ding. Give the woman a star. Yes, of course. It was part of Ron's plan. Get you all in one place. That Marsha and Cindy aren't here is because of the other story I am going to write, and Ron didn't know about. The Harry the Hawk Harrison story. That story is also going to make me a fortune. So it works out for me, but I doubt Ron is happy that two of you aren't here. Still, it's April he wants, and I got her here."

"Here. The police station?"

"Well, duh. Of course. It's about Booker too. He is going to have to choose between April and Bree, and you know which one he is going to choose."

"She's right," April said, standing. "And that is exactly what he should do. Choose Bree. I'm the one that brought this monster into our world. I'm the one who has to take him out of it. Eventually I will. I swear."

"You will not," Judith said.

"I agree," Nicky added, grabbing April's hand. "You can't do this. You know he won't keep his word. He will eliminate Bree just to get her out of his life. There has to be another way."

Ginny laughed. This was going to be such a fantastic story. It would win her fame and fortune. First the story. Then the book. Maybe even a movie. It had everything, and she was right in the middle of it.

It never occurred to Ginny that she was right in the middle of it, because she had to be eliminated, too. Ron had promised her a story. Well, she had one, but she'd never write it. The world would never read it.

Because in order to have the freedom to escape with April, Ron could not let Ginny reveal all that she knew.

So across the street, Ron made the call that would change everything.

Fifty Four

Booker answered, not needing to even look at the phone to know who it was.

"What do you want?"

"You know what I want. April for Bree."

"And you know I can't do that."

"Don't think it's your choice, mate. It's April's. And you know what she is going to choose."

A picture of Bree lying still on what looked like a cellar floor, arms tied behind her back and feet tied together, appeared on his phone.

For a moment, Booker's world turned black, and he thought he would pass out. Gaining control of himself again, he answered, "Still no!"

Two more pictures appeared. A can of gasoline lying beside Bree and a lighter in Ron's hand.

Booker cocked his head, directing the stranger towards his office. With a nod, the man went in and came back holding onto April, and showed Booker that the same pictures had appeared on her phone too.

"Ten minutes. She is coming out that door alone or you all lose everything. Not just Bree. Everything."

The phone went dead.

April felt herself let go of everything she ever wanted. No more crying. No more feeling sorry for herself. She was the only one who could save all her friends, and no one was going to stop her. Trying to pull herself from the stranger's grip, she said, "Let me go. He won't hurt me. Someday I'll get away again. But right now, this is the only answer."

Judith stood behind April, staring at Booker, feeling completely helpless. They had no idea where Ron was, and she knew he would do what he said. Maybe April was right. Maybe it was the only way.

"Who are you?" she asked the man who stood beside Booker and had a grip on April's arm.

"Doesn't matter who I am. Harry sent me. And April, we are going to let you go. Because that is the only way. But it's not how you think it will be."

"And we are supposed to trust you?" Judith demanded, hands on her hips, watching the stranger grip April's arm too tightly.

"For all we know, it's not Harry, who is still in a coma, who sent you, but Ron. Now let April go, or else."

The stranger glanced at Booker, who nodded, and April staggered over into Judith's arms. Nicky watched it all happen through the open office door. She was keeping guard over Ginny, just in case she tried to get away. That would not happen on her watch.

Still, she was terrified. For years she had tracked Ron, always too afraid to deal with him, or even to go to the police, and now they were in a standoff with him. He wanted them to trade one woman they loved for another one they loved.

And nothing that she knew about Ron told her he would keep any bargain he made. So what did he really want?

Ginny laughed, and as if she heard what Nicky was thinking, and said, "Revenge! That's what he wants. And you know as well as I do that he'll get it."

Across the street, Ron didn't give a rat's ass if Booker sent April out. Well, he did. But it didn't matter because he'd get April in the end. He was going to start the fire no matter what. Although he knew revenge would solve nothing, he also knew he would enjoy it while it was happening.

And there was nothing Booker could do to stop it. Ron had more than one fire ready to start. Once the police station started burning, April would escape on her own. She'd understand that's what he wanted her to do. And then with the house on fire across the street, it would be easy for him to grab her and disappear while everyone panicked.

Sure, they knew Bree was in the house. But it would be too late. Even the gentle rain that was now falling wouldn't put it out, but it would help his and April's disappearance.

Once again, the angels were on his side. Well, not the kind with fluffy white wings that only people with muddled brains believed would save them, but the dark ones that served people like him.

"Ready. Set. Go," Ron said, and pushed the first switch. He heard the boom before he saw the flames. It had begun.

Nicky had moved Ginny to the waiting room of the station to join the others, so the explosion in Booker's office didn't kill them, but it distracted everyone long enough that April did just what she knew she was supposed to do. She ran out the front door, knowing she was heading straight into Ron's arms. There was no other way.

As she staggered out into the street, she saw the fire start in the house across from the fire station and knew that was Ron's handiwork, too.

"Bree," she sobbed, and then stopped herself. She could never afford to have another emotion.

A man stepped out from behind the hedge. Ron, it had to be Ron. He grabbed her, pushed her into the car, and was driving down the street within seconds.

In the rearview mirror, Ron saw Booker stagger out of the building and start running towards the speeding car, as if he was superman and could stop the inevitable.

Damn, Ron thought. *It's working*. Booker's Bree was gone, and now he'd have to live with all that guilt and regret. Revenge was sweet.

Turning to April, sitting stoically in the passenger seat, he said, "Put on your seat belt."

And then he pushed the door locks, so she couldn't escape. Not again. Not ever.

Fifty Five

For the rest of their lives, Booker, Judith, and Nicky would remember that moment in time. It would color every decision they ever made. It would wake them up in the middle of the night in cold sweats, and it would alter forever what they believed in.

If they had before believed in the power of good over evil, after that morning, their belief was reinforced. Because as two fires burned—and they thought that one of their beloved friends was burning in one, and the other had been taken away forever by a madman —a vision walked toward them out of the smoke.

Booker, standing in the middle of the street screaming at the car racing away in the distance, heard his name, and turning saw Bree running towards him. He fell to his knees, thinking he had lost his mind. And then Bree was hugging him, and they were sobbing together.

Judith and Nicky stood watching, afraid to move. What if it was all an illusion? How could Bree be alive? The fires across the street and behind them were roaring. They heard the fire engines coming from a few blocks away, but they knew without a doubt that Bree had died in one of those fires, and April was gone forever.

But there was Bree and Booker hugging in the street. And the stranger was holding onto Ginny while talking to a group of men. And then another miracle happened.

A car pulled up, and two more men helped April out of the back seat. Then Judith and Nicky were running and screaming April's name, and they knew it wasn't an illusion. She was real.

Barely aware of what was happening, Nicky, Judith, and April went with the men dressed in black who appeared out of nowhere and ushered them from the middle of the street to a car waiting down the road.

It was only when Amir stepped out of the waiting car that Judith understood what was happening. How it happened, she didn't know. But she knew that somehow Harry had saved her friends' lives.

The stranger who had been in the police station spoke with Booker, and Booker reluctantly helped Bree into the waiting car. Before getting into the car with the rest of them, Judith turned to Booker and waited for an explanation.

When Booker just stood there not able to speak, afraid of breaking down, she broke the silence by asking, "It was Harry, wasn't it?"

Booker sighed and nodded, unaware or uncaring that tears were streaming down his face.

Gesturing at the stranger, he said, "Harry's man. Amir put Harry's plan into action. I don't know much more. Right now, Amir will take you all to the hospital. I need to make sure everyone here is safe and wait until the fire is out before joining you there. Ginny will go with those men for now, since we don't have a jail anymore."

"And Ron?" Judith asked.

Taking Judith by the arm, Booker led her away from the group. Judith steeled herself for the news. "He got away, didn't he?"

The stranger had followed them, and he was the one that answered.

"No ma'am. He didn't. He's on the way to the hospital with life threatening injuries."

For a moment, Judith did the unthinkable. She prayed that he would die.

"What happened?"

"We had the car surrounded. He slipped away and started running. The driver of the firetruck didn't see him."

Sensing Judith's hesitation, the stranger said, "Even if he lives, he will bother none of you ever again."

Judith wanted to say, "How can you be so sure?" but stopped herself in time and thanked him instead.

Booker turned to go, and then came back to Judith and said, "Take care of her for me."

Judith nodded, stood for a moment, and then joined the others in the car. Nicky had her arms around April as they sobbed together. Bree's hands, which had slight burns on them, were being wrapped by another man dressed in black, who was kneeling on the floor in front of her.

Judith slid in beside Amir, but not before looking back at Bree, Nicky, and April, and promising herself she would make sure that Ron never hurt anyone again.

Amir smiled at Judith and whispered, "More good news. Harry is awake."

It was only then, knowing that everyone was okay, that Judith allowed herself to let the tears fall that had been threatening to since the moment she saw Bree walk out of the smoke and into Booker's arms.

"Thank you," she whispered back to Amir. "For all of it."

Amir only nodded and smiled in return.

Judith didn't know how Harry and Amir had saved them, but she would find out. And forever and ever, they would remain treasured members of the Ruby Sister's extended family.

Fifty Six

The first thing Harry had wanted to know when he woke up was if everyone was safe. Judith had called Bruce from the car as Amir drove and filled him in with what they knew, so Bruce could tell Harry that everyone was fine and that they were all on their way to the hospital.

"What did you do?" Bruce asked.

Harry just shook his head, happy to be awake, but so weak he could barely move his hands. He knew that time was short, and he wanted to spend it with Marsha.

"Amir will tell you. But if Bryan hadn't been able to hear me, and pass the message on... well, he's the one to thank. And Bruce, thank you for everything. I'll see you in another lifetime, perhaps."

"I'll be looking for you, my friend," Bruce said, leaning over and kissing Harry's check. "Thank you for teaching me so many things in such a short time."

Marsha hadn't moved, afraid that she would lose Harry if she did. As Bruce closed the door behind him, she sat beside Harry's bed and told him all that she remembered.

He listened, tears running down his cheeks. She had seen him. And remembered. And was grateful.

Harry told Marsha a few stories about her mother that she hadn't known and made her promise that she would forgive her mother for the choices she made. She had thought she was doing the right thing.

Marsha promised. She knew how easy it was to be fooled by circumstances. It would take time, but she would eventually give up her resentment.

Later, Marsha would think of that short time with Harry in the hospital as the happiest moments of her life. Finally, she had accepted that she was loved, and in return, she could love freely. Harry had guessed why her reaction to what he had told her had been out of fear. She was like him. Gay.

"I've always felt like an outcast," Marsha said. "I wanted to be like everyone else."

"You are not an outcast, Marsha. Your friends have always been here for you. And I think they have always known what you were so afraid to tell them. Besides, no one is like anyone else. That's how life works. It's our differences that strengthen us, as a group, a society, the world, and within ourselves. You are strong, my beautiful daughter. All I wish for you is to be yourself and share it with the world."

When Amir arrived, he joined Marsha in the room, and told Harry that all his last wishes were in place.

So when Harry drew his last breath, there was peace in his heart and a smile on his lips, surrounded by two people who loved him.

In the waiting room, Bryan nodded to Harry as he saw him go. Harry didn't need his help anymore. He was shining with light, standing tall as a young man. All his sickness dissolved.

Rachel glanced at Bryan and said, "He's gone, isn't he?"

Turning to everyone waiting to hear, he told them yes, that Harry was happy and well and on his way to his next adventure.

But that was not the only person Bryan saw slip away. However, Harry and Ron were going to two different places. So he told them that too. For Judith, Bruce, Nicky, Cindy and Bree, the reaction was of immense relief. A collective sigh followed Ron as he vanished from their lives.

For April, it was different. All she could feel was a pain so intense she had trouble breathing. She knew it was grief. And she wondered if there was something wrong with her feeling such grief over a man who had done what he had done. But she hadn't known that man. She had known, or thought she had known, another man. Not a perfect husband or father, but neither was she the perfect wife and mother. He had loved her in his own way.

So she grieved for the man she loved, who wasn't the man she thought he was. Grieved for the life she thought she had been living, and the one she thought she would live. All gone.

She grieved for what Ron must have felt lying there in the hospital, alone. Because she had not been allowed in the room. She would have told him she loved the part of him he had discounted and discarded. She had loved who he could have been, and she would have prayed for him to choose a different life next time.

At the same time, she had to admit that she also felt relieved. She could move on with her life without fear. Looking around the hospital waiting room, where all her friends were with her, she smiled through her tears.

Here they were once again in a hospital in a pivotal moment in all their lives. Rho's birth, her recovery after escaping from Ron the first time, and now Harry's and Ron's death had reshaped all their lives in ways they might not have chosen. But they still had each other. That would be enough to rebuild their lives in new and better ways.

And April worried, thinking of her children. They didn't know what had happened. After all of this, would they be okay? Would they be relieved too? Would they also feel grief for what they had thought they had, and then found out they hadn't? And what about Mary and Rho? What would their feelings about Ron become?

Oh, the path of destruction you laid behind you, Ron, April thought, while feeling a flutter of freedom. Ron was done destroying. They were free to move on.

She smiled at her friends, and they all sighed in relief. April would be okay.

Fifty Seven

Harry's death was front page news, but it wasn't Ginny's story. It was a story Harry had prepared, and then Amir gave to the media. There was no mention of Marsha or what happened in Spring Falls. Just that Harry Harrison had passed away in his sleep after a long illness. Most of his fortune having been previously distributed to his favorite charities.

They buried Harry beside Marsha's mother. It had been a small private funeral on a warm cloudy summer day, with only the Ruby Sisters, Booker, Bruce, and Amir attending.

Rachel and Bryan had returned to Doveland before the funeral, after staying with Bree for a few days. It gave them a chance to rest, but it also gave Bree a chance to relive her moments before the fire with Bryan.

She told them she had been afraid that she was going to die. In fact, there were a few moments when she thought she was dead.

"Was it possible that I did die?" Bree asked Bryan.

"What did you see?"

"I saw nothing, really. Just felt a deep sense of calm. I thought the men who were untying me and lifting me out of the basement were an illusion, part of the dream. It was only when we were outside, and they walked me away from the house, and I looked up at the stars that I realized I was still here."

Bryan smiled. "I don't have any answers, Bree. All I know is that there is much more to the visible world than any of us see, and then there is the invisible world, or what some people call other dimensions. Life goes on. That's really all I know for sure."

Before leaving, Bryan and Rachel told the Ruby Sisters that Grace, their friend in Doveland who had introduced them to Rachel and Bryan, hoped that one or all of them would visit them in Doveland sometime. They all promised to think about it, but it was Cindy who wondered if it would be good for her to get away.

At the funeral, she had watched the couples standing together. There were Booker and Bree, Judith and Bruce, Marsha and Nicky, who obviously were still thinking they were just friends. Only she and April stood alone. But April had family. She had no one other than the Ruby Sisters. Would they have time for her in the future as they built new lives?

Cindy had wanted to slap herself for those thoughts. She had everything she could ever want. A business she loved that Mimi and Janet ran with as much care as if it were their own. She had the Ruby Sisters and the men who loved them. She even had a beautiful god-daughter to love.

Really. What was wrong with her? So she smiled and was grateful, but inside she felt a grief for something that had not happened—her life as an artist. And she knew it never would. But she kept that to herself, as she always did.

After the funeral, April had asked Booker about Ginny, another person April had trusted who had turned out not to be someone she claimed to be. But April still cared about what happened to her.

"I wouldn't worry about her," Booker said. "A few years in jail. A book in her head and time to write it. She'll be fine."

April bowed her head, hoping Ginny would find her better self and do good in the world after her experience with them. Maybe they had rubbed off on her somehow. April was determined to not let who Ginny was and what she had done change how she saw the world. Thinking everyone was out to get her would not make her a pleasant person to be around, and she'd never find her joy again.

Ron did not have a funeral. April had asked Booker and Bruce to handle the arrangements for his body. Someday she'd find out what they had done, but she didn't want to know yet. And Ron didn't deserve more. Still, he had been her husband, and she would mourn him more fully someday. Just not now.

After Harry's funeral, they gathered in Judith's living room and Amir shared how Harry, afraid something like that would happen after learning about Ron, had hired the men that rescued April and Bree.

Amir told them he would return home to be with his wife, who had waited patiently for him to give her his full attention, but first he had a few things to carry out that Harry had asked him to do.

Reaching into the bag he had brought with him, Amir pulled out a huge scrapbook and handed it to Marsha.

Opening it, she saw it was filled with everything that had marked her life. She saw a clipping from the newspaper of her first performance in nursery school where she had sung Mary Had A Little Lamb for their graduation ceremony before kindergarten.

Flipping quickly through the book, she saw her last performance in New York, and the pictures of her students' recitals once she moved away and started teaching.

On the last page was a picture of April's house, and in handwriting she could barely read, it said, "I wish I could be here for the grand opening, but I know you will make this into something beautiful."

What Marsha wanted to do was break down into sobs, she but held it back. This wasn't the time for sorrow. This was a time for gratitude for what she had been given. She vowed to honor Harry by making sure they had a grand opening.

Closing the scrapbook, she passed it to Judith, and then watched it make its way around the room to return to her. Each person smiling and crying as they flipped through the pages.

Once it returned to Marsha, Amir stood and said, "One last thing," while taking the envelope out of his jacket pocket he had so carefully watched over the last few weeks.

"Harry asked me to give you all these necklaces once he was gone. He loved that you all found each other and stayed together, and the name you gave yourselves. He said these are not a replacement for the red glass bauble Cindy gave you when you were in grade school, or the necklace Paul gave you, Bree. They are an addition, and a reminder that you are one for all, just in case anyone might forget. And as you already know, rubies are a symbol of love and courage, and all of you have those two qualities in abundance."

Going to each Ruby Sister, he asked them to stand, and then put on each of their necks a slender gold necklace with a beautiful ruby pendant. Bree's necklace from Paul lay perfectly within the circle of the necklace from Harry.

As they stood together, the sun broke through the clouds, sending streaks of light into the living room, glancing off the rubies, filling the room with a light none of them had ever seen before.

"Thank you, Harry," they all whispered.

Fifty Eight

A few days later, Marsha and April sat against the wall of the downstairs room of the Ruby House, legs outstretched, watching the light dance through the leaves of the maple tree.

With the windows open, they could hear the birds and the tinkling of the wind chimes that Nicky had given them before she returned home, promising she'd be back and reminding them they were always welcome to visit her and Sara.

Marsha had been tempted to ask Nicky not to leave, but knew it was too soon. For both of them. They both had healing to do, and then they could decide if there was more to the two of them.

But just knowing that it would be okay if that's what happened had thrilled them both. It was unfamiliar territory. Neither one of them had let themselves believe it was possible to have a life like other people. Time would tell what would happen, and they were both content with that.

As they sat in silence, Marsha was waiting for what April had to tell her, fairly sure it wasn't a good thing. That morning April had a meeting with Judith and Booker, and returned looking more tired and depressed than she had ever seen her.

Finally, when April said nothing, and Marsha itched to be up and doing something, she said, "It can't be that bad."

"Oh. It could be."

Marsha pulled her legs in, turned to face April, and reached out to hold her hand.

"Well, whatever it is, we'll cross it together. After all, we're roommates now."

The two of them had moved into the upstairs rooms of the Ruby House, deciding that it was time to get started on their vision of what it could be. Everything was in place. Seth had the plans, and they had hired the video crew.

They could have waited. After all, both of them had just had someone they loved die. At first, they thought maybe it was wrong to move forward, but then both Ron and Harry had wanted this house for them.

So while mourning the Ron she had loved most of her life, and Harry, who Marsha had loved only for a few days, they would rebuild their lives by transforming the Ruby House.

They'd turn it into a place where joy lived. In fact, that was going to be their logo. A sign that said, "Where Joy Lives" was being made and would hang over the front door as it welcomed the people who came to the dance and theatre studio.

Until her meeting with Judith and Booker, April had been filled with excitement about the project. But now she could barely lift her head to look at Marsha.

"Come on April. What is it?"

Dropping her head even lower, April said so softly that Marsha could barely hear her, "Ron's money is gone. All of it. Well, most of it. They took it all away. Booker tried to explain why. But I don't understand. It doesn't matter, anyway. I get to keep the house, and the money that I saved in my account, but that's barely enough to keep the house running, let alone fix it up and build what we wanted to build."

Marsha laughed. She didn't intend for that to happen. But it did. Laughter bubbled up out of her, pulling her to her feet, spilling across the floor and out into the world. It was a marvel. She was laughing. *When was the last time she laughed,* she wondered. It felt wonderful. She'd have to do more of it.

April stood and looked at Marsha as if she had gone crazy.

"What's the matter with you? Don't you understand? I'm broke? I'll have to sell this house. We can't do this dream. It's just one more thing that Ron ruined for me. And you."

Marsha stopped laughing, but still felt the joy that had erupted bubbling up inside of her. "Oh April. Don't you know? Didn't Judith tell you?"

"She tried to tell me something, but I rushed out the door."

Marsha took April's hands and said, "You may not be rich anymore, April. But I am. Rich enough to do all of this, and much more."

"Harry?" April asked, the color returning to her face.

Marsha nodded, and the two of them walked to the window, gazing out at the town they loved, and smiled.

When Seth pulled up and waved at them, they waved back, and he wondered what had made Marsha look like a glowing light.

Marsha danced across the floor to greet him, dragging April with her.

"Come on, girl, we have work to do! And no more time to waste."

As April giggled the way she used to when they were kids, Marsha felt as if her heart would burst with happiness. And although she had seen how sad Cindy had looked at the funeral, she wasn't worried. They'd face whatever was bothering Cindy together.

After all, Marsha thought, this was the place that joy lives, in this house, and in her heart, and she had enough to share with everyone.

Author Note

I named the character Ginny Lynn after a long-time friend. Her name was Ginny Lynn Safford, and she was an angel to me. Long ago, she gave me a place to stay when I was homeless. She hired me to choreograph for a theatre piece she was producing, reminding me who I am. She taught me how to say phrases instead of run-on sentences, helped me lower my voice so I didn't sound like a squeaky mouse when I was doing sales presentations.

Ginny Lynn was a wonderful friend who only wanted the best for everyone she knew. She was nothing like the Ginny Lynn in this story. Even though many years have gone by since she passed away, relocated to another place in Life, I think of her often. To that Ginny, I send love and gratitude.

Ginny Lynn is just one of the many amazing women I know and have known. I know what women can do when they band together in harmony and courage. This is one reason I thoroughly love writing this series. Women's friendship, courage, compassion, and inspiration have guided me in my life. I hope that the women—and men who love and support them—in these books will provide comfort and inspiration to my readers.

Thank you for reading my books. It is for you that I write. ~ Beca

PS: Did you enjoy meeting Rachel and Bryan? They are visitors from the book series, *Stories From Doveland*. You can read their story in the stand-alone book *In-Between*.

Watch for the next book in this series, *As If It Was Real*. Learn more about all the Ruby Sisters and their friends, while discovering more about Cindy's life.

Also By Beca

The Ruby Sisters Series: Women's Lit, Friendship
A Last Gift, After All This Time, And Then She Remembered, As
If It Was Real...

Stories From Doveland: Magical Realism, Friendship
Karass, Pragma, Jatismar, Exousia, Stemma, Paragnosis,
In-Between, Missing, Out Of Nowhere

The Return To Erda Series: Fantasy
Shatterskin, Deadsweep, Abbadon, The Experiment

The Chronicles of Thamon: Fantasy
Banished, Betrayed, Discovered, Wren's Story

The Shift Series: Spiritual Self-Help
Living in Grace: The Shift to Spiritual Perception
The Daily Shift: Daily Lessons From Love To Money
The 4 Essential Questions: Choosing Spiritually Healthy Habits
The 28 Day Shift To Wealth: A Daily Prosperity Plan

The Intent Course: Say Yes To What Moves You
Imagination Mastery: A Workbook For Shifting Your Reality
Right Thinking: A Thoughtful System for Healing
Perception Mastery: Seven Steps To Lasting Change
Blooming Your Life: How To Experience Consistent Happiness

Perception Parables: Very short stories
Love's Silent Sweet Secret: A Fable About Love
Golden Chains And Silver Cords: A Fable About Letting Go

Advice:
A Woman's ABC's of Life: Lessons in Love, Life, and Career from
Those Who Learned The Hard Way
The Daily Nudge(s): So When Did You First Notice

Acknowledgements

I could never write a book without the help of my friends and my book community. Thank you, Jet Tucker, Jamie Lewis, Barbara Budan, and Diana Cormier for taking the time to do the final reader proof. You are a loyal and much-loved reader team. You can't imagine how much I appreciate it.

A huge thank you to Laura Moliter for her fantastic book editing.

Thank you to every other member of my Book Community who helps me make so many decisions that help the book be the best book possible.

Thank you to all the people who tell me they love to read these stories. Those random comments from friends and strangers are more valuable than gold.

And as always, thank you to my beloved husband, Del, for being my daily sounding board, for putting up with all my questions, my constant need to want to make things better, and for being the love of my life, in more than just this one lifetime.

Connect with me online:

Facebook: https://www.facebook.com/becalewiscreative
Instagram: https://instagram.com/becalewis
TikTok: https://tiktok.com/@becalewis
Twitter: http://twitter.com/becalewis
LinkedIn: https://linkedin.com/in/becalewis
Youtube: https://www.youtube.com/c/becalewis

About Beca

Beca writes books she hopes will change people's perceptions of themselves and the world, and open possibilities to things and ideas that are waiting to be seen and experienced.

At sixteen, Beca founded her own dance studio. Later, she received a Master's Degree in Dance in Choreography from UCLA and founded the Harbinger Dance Theatre, a multimedia dance company, while continuing to run her dance school.

After graduating—to better support her three children—Beca switched to the sales field, where she worked as an employee and independent contractor to many industries, excelling in each while perfecting and teaching her Shift System® and writing books.

She joined the financial industry in 1983 and became an Associate Vice President of Investments at a major stock brokerage firm, and was a licensed Certified Financial Planner for over twenty years.

This diversity, along with a variety of life challenges, helped fuel the desire to share what she's learned by writing and speaking, hoping it will make a difference in other people's lives.

BECA LEWIS

Beca grew up in State College, PA, with the dream of becoming a dancer and then a writer. She carried that dream forward as she fulfilled a childhood wish by moving to Southern California in 1968. Beca told her family she would never move back to the cold.

After living there for thirty-one years, she met her husband Delbert Lee Piper, Sr., at a retreat in Virginia, and everything changed. They decided to find a place they could call their own, which sent them off traveling around the United States. They lived and worked in a few different places before returning to live in the cold once again near Del's family in a small town in Northeast Ohio, not too far from State College.

When not working and teaching together, they love to visit and play with their combined family of eight children and five grandchildren, read, study, do yoga or taiji, feed birds, and work in their garden.